VS

VOL.
1

→FRONT
TOWARDS
ENEMY_

ORIGINALLY
PUBLISHED
AS VS #1-5

VS

VOL. 1

→ SCRIPT: IVÁN BRANDON

• ART: ESAD RIBIĆ

• COLOR ART: NIC KLEIN

→ WITH IVE SVORCINA & EM ROBERTS (CHAPTER 5)

→VS CREATED BY
IVÁN BRANDON & ESAD RIBIĆ

- LETTERING: ADITYA BIDIKAR
- BRANDING/PUBLICATION DESIGN/ IN-WORLD GRAPHICS: TOM MULLER

↓

- EDITOR: SEBASTIAN GIRNER
- COVER ARTIST: ESAD RIBIĆ

- PRODUCTION ARTIST: SHANNA MATUSZAK

[3D CHERRY COMBAT ART: TIM MULLER]

INFO MESSAGE

VS
■
VOL.
1
●

→FR
TOWA
EN

ONT
RDS
EMY_

LOADING:
TONIGHT'S
WAR
DX ANNOUNCEMENT
CHAPTER 1

QUIET.

WHAT DO YOU HEAR?
NOTHING.

NOTHING...

I CAN'T ABIDE A SILENCE.

FIORINO, WHERE *ARE* THEY?
ONE KLICK SOUTH-SOUTHWEST.
THEY'RE COMING FOR US.
ZZZZZT..

BEIN' *WATCHED.*
WE'RE *ALWAYS* BEING WATCHED.
BIM AND SONNY, FAN *OUT*, 87 ZED. DON'T MAKE IT EASY ON THEM.
ALL THE REST KEEP TIGHT ON *ME*.
FFFFSSS
DON'T MAKE IT EASY, HE SAYS...

I GOT EYES ON THEM.
THEY'RE... *WAITING?*
THAT'S NO GOOD.
NO. BRING THEM *AROUND,* DALEY.
I WOULD *LOVE* TO.
EASY NOW...
WE'RE TOO EXPOSED HERE, STAY WHERE YOU--

MOTHERXXXX!
CHU'S DOWN!
I'M ON YOUR SHOOTER.
WEAPONS FREE.
I NEED BACKUP, THEY'RE HERE!
HKK
FWOO FWOO
WE GOT THEIR CAP.
NGK
OUR COVER'S COOKED, WE NEED...
FWM

BOOM
I GOT YOU.
FWOOO
NEED SPEAKERS ON THIS THING.
SOMETHING ORCHESTRAL. DEATH FROM ABOVE.
OH, XXXX.
FTOFTOFTO FTOFTO
DO DO DOM
CRASH AND BURN, YOU RANCID--AAGH!
BEHIND US. HOW ARE THEY BEHIND--?
BOOOM

YOU HAVE THE RIGHT TO SURRENDER. BY THE TERMS OF ARTICLE 18 VEGA.
I WAS BEHIND *YOU*. HOW DID YOU--?
VID ERROR.
3-MINUTE WAR DELAY.
WHAT?!
WE WILL RETURN TO THE CONFLICT SHORTLY.
WAR DELAY?

I WILL WALK ON YOUR EYES.
TECHNICAL FOUL
PLAYER:
"MAMA" MARTINEZ
YOU WILL SIT DOWN, NOW.
AND THEN AGAIN NEXT WEEK AND THE NEXT AGAIN.
MAMA. STOP.
WE WERE THERE, FLYNN! ONE SECOND LEFT!
AND NOW WE'RE NOT. AND EVERY BATXXXX WORD YOU SAY NOW PUSHES US FURTHER AWAY.
YOU WANT THE WHOLE THING FORFEIT?
SUBSTITUTION
TURN OUT THEIR LIGHTS, FLYNN.
PLAYER: KREBS
HAS JOINED THE FRONT LINES
LIEUTENANT?
19 FLUSH, KREBS. WATCH THE CORNERS.
Don't forget to join us Tuesday night for our RETURN TO SPARTA!
Brought to you by:
Eternity Mobile Gravesites

YOU *SEE* HIM, KREBS? THAT'S ALL YOU DO, *SEE* HIM. THEN GO AND KNOCK HIM DOWN.
THAT'S THE *HEEL*. THAT'S WHERE THEY'RE DIGGING IN.
YOU UNDER-STAND ME?
KNOCK HIM DOWN.
PERFECTLY STATED, KREBS.
YOU'VE GOT YOUR MARKS.
RISE UP, LEGION!
AND SHOW THE BOTTOMS OF YOUR FEET!
I'LL SHUT HIS MOUTH.

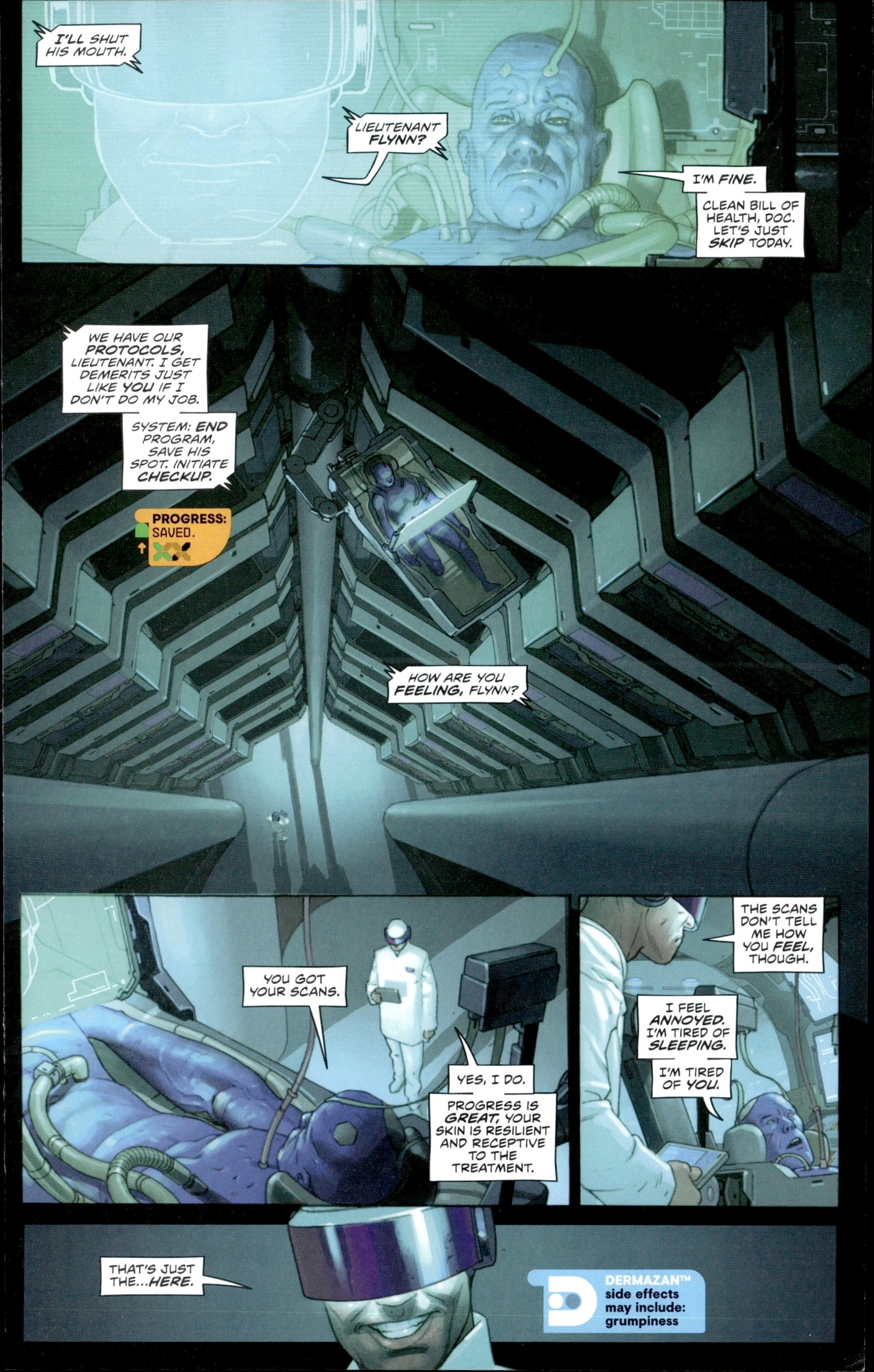
I'LL SHUT HIS MOUTH.
LIEUTENANT FLYNN?
I'M FINE.
CLEAN BILL OF HEALTH, DOC. LET'S JUST SKIP TODAY.
WE HAVE OUR PROTOCOLS, LIEUTENANT. I GET DEMERITS JUST LIKE YOU IF I DON'T DO MY JOB.
SYSTEM: END PROGRAM, SAVE HIS SPOT. INITIATE CHECKUP.
PROGRESS: SAVED.
HOW ARE YOU FEELING, FLYNN?
YOU GOT YOUR SCANS.
YES, I DO.
PROGRESS IS GREAT, YOUR SKIN IS RESILIENT AND RECEPTIVE TO THE TREATMENT.
THE SCANS DON'T TELL ME HOW YOU FEEL, THOUGH.
I FEEL ANNOYED. I'M TIRED OF SLEEPING.
I'M TIRED OF YOU.
THAT'S JUST THE...HERE.
DERMAZAN™ side effects may include: grumpiness

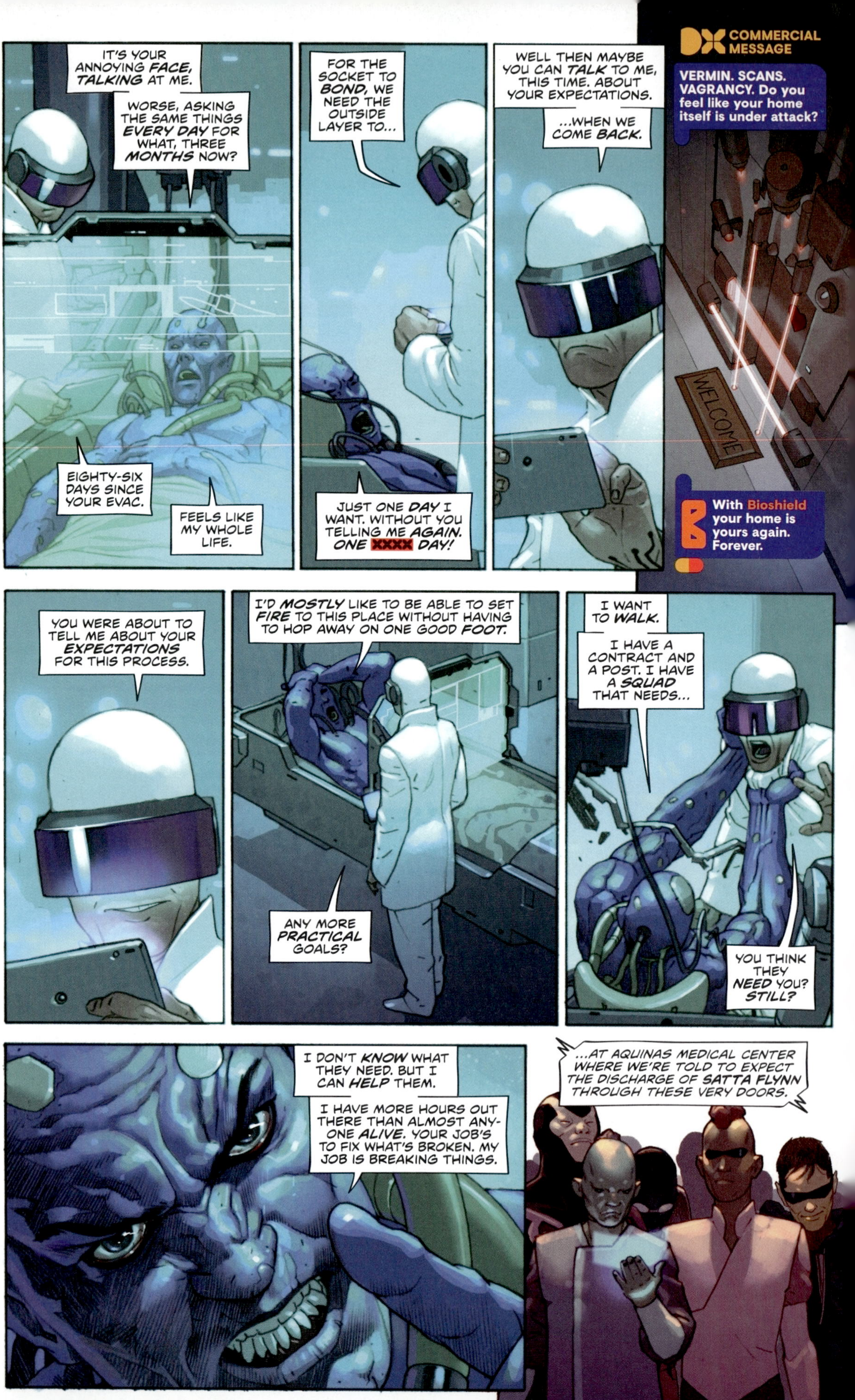
IT'S YOUR ANNOYING FACE, TALKING AT ME.
WORSE, ASKING THE SAME THINGS EVERY DAY FOR WHAT, THREE MONTHS NOW?
EIGHTY-SIX DAYS SINCE YOUR EVAC.
FEELS LIKE MY WHOLE LIFE.
FOR THE SOCKET TO BOND, WE NEED THE OUTSIDE LAYER TO...
JUST ONE DAY I WANT. WITHOUT YOU TELLING ME AGAIN. ONE XXXX DAY!
WELL THEN MAYBE YOU CAN TALK TO ME, THIS TIME. ABOUT YOUR EXPECTATIONS.
...WHEN WE COME BACK.
DX COMMERCIAL MESSAGE
VERMIN. SCANS. VAGRANCY. Do you feel like your home itself is under attack?
WELCOME
With Bioshield your home is yours again. Forever.
YOU WERE ABOUT TO TELL ME ABOUT YOUR EXPECTATIONS FOR THIS PROCESS.
I'D MOSTLY LIKE TO BE ABLE TO SET FIRE TO THIS PLACE WITHOUT HAVING TO HOP AWAY ON ONE GOOD FOOT.
ANY MORE PRACTICAL GOALS?
I WANT TO WALK.
I HAVE A CONTRACT AND A POST. I HAVE A SQUAD THAT NEEDS...
YOU THINK THEY NEED YOU? STILL?
I DON'T KNOW WHAT THEY NEED. BUT I CAN HELP THEM.
I HAVE MORE HOURS OUT THERE THAN ALMOST ANY-ONE ALIVE. YOUR JOB'S TO FIX WHAT'S BROKEN. MY JOB IS BREAKING THINGS.
...AT AQUINAS MEDICAL CENTER WHERE WE'RE TOLD TO EXPECT THE DISCHARGE OF SATTA FLYNN THROUGH THESE VERY DOORS.

INFO MESSAGE
Lieutenant Flynn of the industrial guard was injured in the War of the Seven Fires back in the Spring.
In a speech earlier today, Flynn's lead doctor called his condition: "better now than at his peak".
FLYNN!
FLYNN!!
FLYNN!
OVER HERE!
YOU GONNA LET US OUT OR GONNA STAND THERE LIKE A LOGJAM?
LIEUTENANT FLYNN ONLY HAS TIME FOR A FEW QUESTIONS, OKAY? LET'S TRY TO SAVE YOUR STINKERS FOR NEXT TIME.
THE BIGGEST QUESTION TODAY, FLYNN...
...HOW DOES IT FEEL BACK ON YOUR FEET?
WELP...
HHN
YOU'RE NOT SUPPOSED TO STAND UNTIL...
LET'S SEE, HUH?
FEELS PRETTY GOOD.

THIS IS A MIRACLE! I CAN'T BELIEVE IT.
EXCUSE ME...
LET XEM THROUGH.
THE THINGS YOU BEEN THROUGH, IT'S A MIRACLE. I PRAYED THE WHOLE TIME FOR THIS.
I WANNA TOUCH FLYNN, TOO!
IN THERE IT'S HARD TO KEEP YOUR HEAD.
WITHOUT YOU ALL OUT HERE I COULDN'T MAKE IT THROUGH.
EVER IN YOUR SERVICE!
FLYNN, TAKE ME WITH YOU, TOO!
YOU LOOK A LITTLE PALE.
THIS THING'S EXCRUCIATING.
WHERE DOES IT HURT?
WHERE THE NUB MEETS THE CONDUIT.

TOLDYA WE SHOULDA SHAVED DOWN MORE OF THAT LEG.
WE'RE NOT REMOVING *MORE* OF HIM FOR THE SAKE OF YOUR *TECH!*
IT'S A *STUMP!* WHAT'S IT TO *HIM* HOW *LONG* A STUMP IT IS?! HE'S A *SOLDIER!*
HE CAN'T BE HOBBLING AROUND!
HE'LL DO WHAT'S *NEEDED.* LIKE HE ALWAYS HAS.
CUT THEM *BOTH* OFF, FOR ALL I CARE.
BUT GET ME ON THAT LINE.
OVERDUE COMMERCIAL BREAK
SSHHHH
SIGH
"TIMES LIKE THESE I NEED A *COLD* ONE."
DX COMMERCIAL MESSAGE
CHERRY COMBAT
For times like these.

IT'S NOT YOUR SECOND COMING, SATTA. YOU'RE AT THE PEAK ALREADY. RIGHT WHERE YOU WERE.
LET'S KEEP OUR EXPECTATIONS GROUNDED.

YOU STICK TO YOUR WORLD, DOC. I KNOW WHAT FLYNN CAN DO.
WELL, I CAN QUANTIFY, DOWN TO THE DECIMAL...

HE CAN'T EVEN HEAR YOU, SEE. HE AIN'T EVEN HERE.

SHE'S RIGHT.
FLYNN? CAN YOU HEAR MY VOICE?
WISH TO THE HEAVENLY BODY I COULD LEARN THAT TRICK.
WE'RE BACK IN FIVE. FOUR. THREE.
SATTA FLYNN, LOOKING LIKE HE COULD END THIS WHOLE THING WITH HIS EYES.
WE DO THIS FAST.
TWO
ONE
BAM
BAM
BAM
WE'VE GOT A GRAND FINALE COMING UP...

BOO BOO BOO
WE'VE GOT SOME UNEXPECTED FIRE FROM THE CENTURION SIDE...
UGH, I JINXED IT, DIDN'T I.
I NEED A SITREP, WHERE'S THAT FIRE COMING FROM...
WHO'S EVEN LEFT?
I SEE H--KKK!
MASTODON'S VITALS JUST WENT FLAT.
I MET HIM YEARS BACK ON HIS FIRST TOUR.
YOU WERE THE REAL DEAL, BUDDY.
CHENG, WE GOT A MASHER ON YOUR BACK.
MY EYES ARE OPEN.
AND THESE GUYS ARE SLOW.
IT'S NOT ABOUT SPEED.
LEGIONARY CHENG IS OFF THE BOARD.
IN LIEU OF PROTO-FLOWERS, CHENG ASKED FOR CONTRIBUTIONS MADE TO THE EASTERN LEGION'S YOUTH FOUNDATION.

PRESSING FORWARD WITHOUT BACKUP. THIS IS VINTAGE SATTA FLYNN WE'RE SEEING.
WE NEED A TIME OUT!
HE'S CREEPING 'ROUND!
WE DON'T NEED XXXX. I'VE WATCHED HIS VID. HE'S A LIMP XXXX FROM THIS RANGE.
BATATATATA
IMPRESSIVE SPACING ON THOSE SHOTS. LEGION PUTTING ON QUITE A SHOW AFTER A DIFFICULT FIRST HALF.
BEAUTIFUL CLUSTER. SERIOUSLY.
FALL BACK! FALL BAAAAACK!

NO...
FT
NOW YOU FALL DOWN.
SATTA FLYNN DISARMED! WHAT A NIGHT!
C'MON, HE'S NEVER DISARMED.
SPLAT

WATCHED ALL YOUR VIDS. I KNOW YOUR TIMING.
KNOW YOUR THREE MOVES FROM THERE.
EVERY GREAT WARRIOR MUST ONE DAY LEAVE THE FIELD.
THIS IS MY FIELD.

A VETERAN SPIKE BY FLYNN. INSTANT FLATLINE.
BUT WATCH THAT LEFT!
WARNING
FLYNN'S VITALS DIVING NOW. HE HIT AN ARTERY.
SITREP...
WARNING
FLYNN'S TEMPERATURE'S DROPPING. WE MIGHT NOT HAVE A WIN TONIGHT.
WARNING
WARNING
COELUM NOBISCUM!
SATTA FLYNN'S WHOLE LEFT SIDE IS FLASHING RED LIGHTS.
IF HE'S STILL BREATHING IN THE MORNING, OUR MED-POLLS SHOW A LIKELIHOOD OF PERMANENT NERVE DAMAGE...
"COELUM NOBISCUM" SEEMS TO BE A VARIATION ON A PRE-CELESTIAL BATTLE PHRASE. A FULL DEFINITION, AND OUR EPIC FINAL STANDOFF AFTER THIS BRIEF WORD FROM EXOTIC CLIMATES™.

WHUMKK
WE...LEAVE THIS FIELD... TOGETHER.
PENALTY
PLAYER: SATTA FLYNN
SATTA FLYNN WITH A FLAGRANT PROMOTIONAL VIOLATION.
OUR APOLOGIES TO THE AUDIENCE AND TO TONIGHT'S SPONSORS.
YOUR...GLORY... JOINS YOU...IN... THE NEXT PLACE.
OUR FINAL SCAN BEFORE THE BREAK SHOWS NO SURVIVING LEGIONARIES.
YOUR... GLORY...

I GUESS IT'S VICTORY FOR FLYNN AND THE SURVIVING INDUSTRIAL GUARD.
MORE TO COME!
We'll be back after these messages.

COMMERCIAL MESSAGE
CHERRY COMBAT
CHERRY FLAVORED BEVERAGE

CHERRY
COMBAT

CHERRY FLAVORED BEVERAGE

For times like these.

OFFICIAL SPONSOR OF
THE INDUSTRIAL GUARD

LOADING:
TONIGHT'S WAR
DX ANNOUNCEMENT
CHAPTER 2

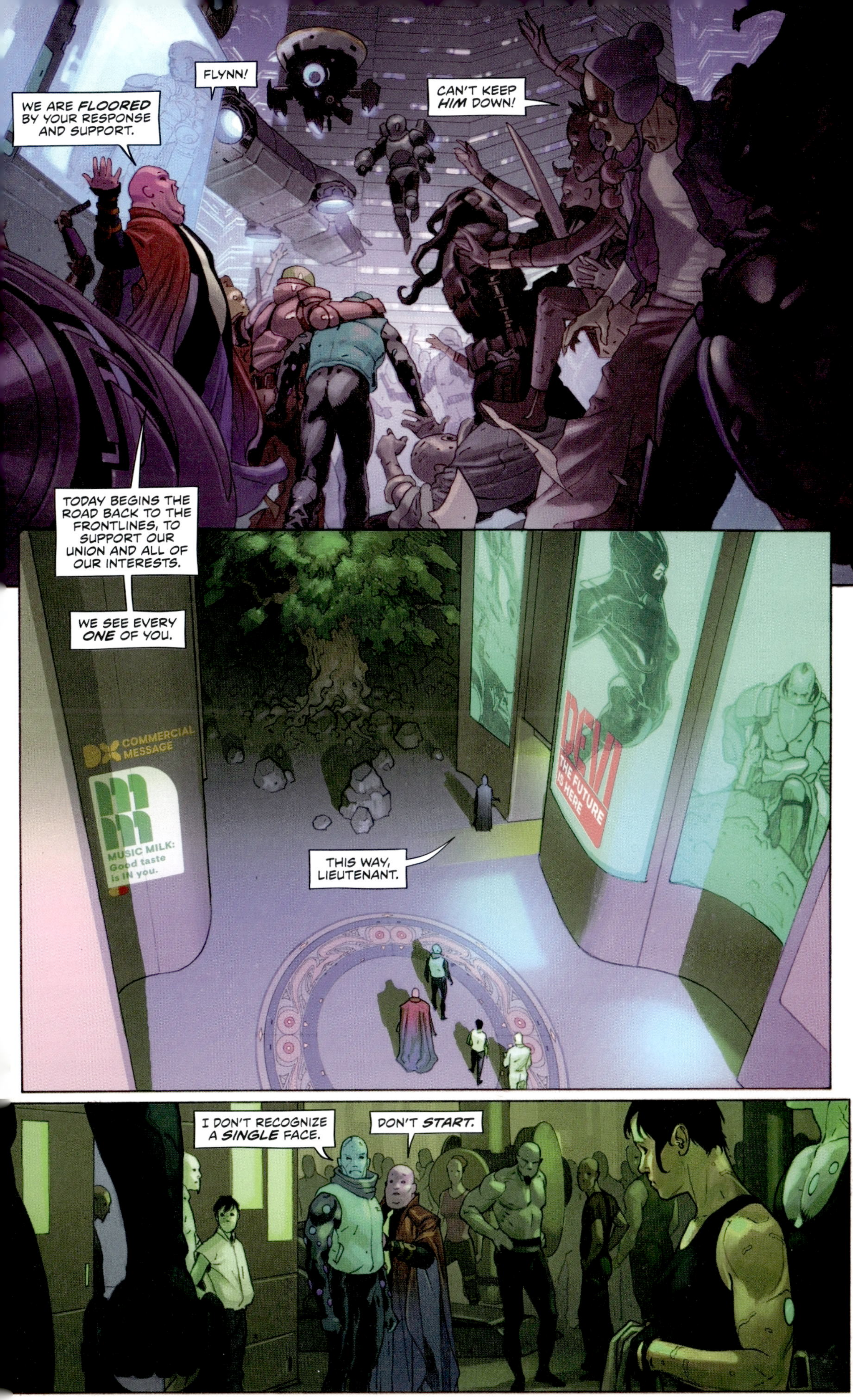
WE ARE FLOORED BY YOUR RESPONSE AND SUPPORT.
FLYNN!
CAN'T KEEP HIM DOWN!
TODAY BEGINS THE ROAD BACK TO THE FRONTLINES, TO SUPPORT OUR UNION AND ALL OF OUR INTERESTS.
WE SEE EVERY ONE OF YOU.
COMMERCIAL MESSAGE
MUSIC MILK: Good taste is IN you.
DEVI
THE FUTURE IS HERE
THIS WAY, LIEUTENANT.
I DON'T RECOGNIZE A SINGLE FACE.
DON'T START.

START WHAT?
LOOK AT WHAT'S LEFT OF THIS, THE SQUAD. IT'S ME, BASICALLY.
LOOK AT WHAT'S LEFT OF YOU.
I SAW MAMA IN HERE SOMEWHERE.
ROOM LOOKS PRETTY FULL TO ME.
ALRIGHT, I DON'T WANT TO WASTE A LOT OF TIME WITH INTRODUCTIONS. LET'S LEARN WHO WE ARE THROUGH OUR ACTIONS ON THE FIELD. LET'S DIVE IN DEEP, MANEUVER EPSILON--
LET'S KEEP THAT CHATTER TO A MINIMUM. EASY COMPANY, STRAFE AND RUN. ON MY GO.
BIG DAY FOR OUR MILITARY TODAY, AS THE LEGENDARY SATTA FLYNN RETURNS TO TRAIN FOR THE BATTLE OF ALCAZAR.
LIEUTENANT FLYNN WAS PLACED ONTO THE DL BACK IN Q2 AFTER EXTREME TIBIOFEMORAL DAMAGE TO HIS LEFT WALKER IN THE WAR OF THE SEVEN FIRES.

ALCAZAR PITS THE TROOPS AGAINST THE EMPIRE OF THE NEW DAY, WHO ARE ON A RECORD-BREAKING RUN SINCE Q3, FIVE CYCLES AGO.
SOMEBODY HELP, SOMEBODY *PLEASE!*
THIS BATTLE'S VICTOR WILL RETAIN ALL TELETALK RIGHTS FOR THE MARSH DISTRICT.
POLICE! YOU CAN'T LET THEM DO THIS! I HAVE MY RIGHTS!
IT'S A RECORD RUN, BUT OUR INDUSTRIAL GUARD HAVE NEVER LOST IN THEIR OWN BACKYARD.
NOTICE
-1919
YOU HAVE A NEGATIVE BALANCE. YOU ARE EXPERIENCING A SERVICE INTERRUPTION.
I AUTHORIZE IMMEDIATE PAYMENT OF 4700 CREDS TO THE PEOPLE'S ENFORCEMENT SERVICE.
A LATE PROCESSING FEE WILL APPLY.

WAR-RELATED PRAYER IS AT A QUARTERLY HIGH, BASED PRESUMABLY ON THE EXCEPTIONAL STAKES OF THIS CONTEST.
THOSE TELETALK RIGHTS COULD BOOST THE INDUSTRIAL PUBLIC'S FLACCID ECONOMY BACK TO WHERE IT WAS DURING THE **NEW GOLD RUSH** OF THE SECOND WAVE.
AS USUAL WE KNOW THE OVERSIGHT METEOR IS **LISTENING...**
BUT WILL IT **HEAR** THEIR PRAYERS?

SPEAKING OF PRAYING, THE PUBLIC™ HAS TO BE PRAYING TONIGHT OVER THE DEBUT OF THEIR NEWEST PRIVATE CHANNEL TEAM, BLACK BOX 7.
DX COMMERCIAL MESSAGE
With PRAYERBOOST, all your pleas get top priority.
I'M HEARING CRAZY THINGS ABOUT THIS NEW TEAM. THE BRASS ARE CALLING THIS THE SECOND COMING.
BUT SKEPTICS SAY THE MONEY THEY'VE SPENT ON TRAINING AND DEVELOPMENT HAS LEFT THEM SET FOR COLLAPSE RIGHT OUT OF THE GATE.
I THINK IT'S SO EXCITING. THIS NEW WORLD MOVES SO FAST! MAYBE POOR FLYNN'S COME BACK TO FIND HIMSELF OBSOLETE!
NOTHING REPLACES A CLASSIC, JANE. FLYNN IS ARGUABLY THE GREATEST TO EVER WEAR THE DOG TAGS.

SKY BEEN LIKE THIS LONG?
SINCE THEY LAUNCHED THIS SETPIECE.
THEY PIPE THE WEATHER IN. "FACTIONS GO UP AGAINST EACH OTHER AND THE ELEMENTS!"
YOU READY, FLYNN?
IT DOESN'T MATTER NOW.
ARE YOU READY, FOLKS AT HOME? WHEN YOU HEAR THAT BELL...
DX COMMERCIAL MESSAGE
Today's drop brought to you by STYX afterlife cosmetics

THIS.
MEANS.
WAR!
I LOVE THAT SOUND.

VERICA'S HIT!
PRESS FORWARD!
I GOT YOUR COVER, LT.
YOU ALWAYS DO, MAMA.
GIVE HIM A HERO'S DEATH.
HE'S GOT ME, I CAN'T LINE IT UP...

YOU CALL FOR BACKUP?
NO!
DAMN IT, I HAD THEM BOTH!
NEED YOU ON FOOT, LIEUTENANT.
SEVEN, MOVE IN.
SIR, YES SIR!

BRATT BRAAAT
TANAKA'S PINNED DOWN BUT HE'S SLIPPERY.
WHOEVER TAGS HIM GETS A WEEK OF SHORE LEAVE.
WHAT ARE WE DOING? WE NEED TO GET SOMEONE BEHIND HIM...
THIS GUY IS FAST.
BRAT
DID HE JUST JUMP THAT LEDGE ON PURPOSE?
I STILL HAVE EYES ON HIM. CYRUS, STOMP HIM OUT.

KRUNK
DON'T HAVE TO TELL ME TWI--
BRRATATRA
BRATATATA
WE GOT HEAVY METAL, FIRE AT WILL!
HOLD YOUR FIRE! HOLD YOUR FIRE!

A LITTLE FRIENDLY FIRE ON THE INDUSTRIAL SIDE...
SHIT. SHIT.
WHO'S GIVING ORDERS TONIGHT?
...
WHERE ARE MY NUMBER 3 ROUNDS?!
ON THE WAY!
HELLO, CAVALRY! THE EMPIRE IS BACK IN THIS.

PRESS IN! THIS IS YOUR DAY!
UH, MA'AM?
BRUTAL TAKE-DOWN BY THIS BLACK BOX TEAM.
THAT STUN GOOP'S EFFECTS ARE PRETTY UPSETTING.

BOFF
BOFF
BOFF
FORWARD GUARD!
OSHINOMI DOWN.
AND MICHIYO! I REALLY LIKED HER.
WHO'S LEFT, YANAGI?

I THINK SHE HEARD YOU! YANAGI'S OFF THE BOARD.
BUT WE FORGOT ABOUT TANAKA!
LOOKS LIKE FLYNN DIDN'T FORGET.
HIS TRACKS JUST...END?

OUR CLOCK IS RUNNING OUT.
IF TANAKA MAKES IT TO THE FLAG BEFORE THE BUZZER...
SERGEANT, CALL TIME. MISSION COMPLETED.
ONE HOUR, NINE MINUTES.

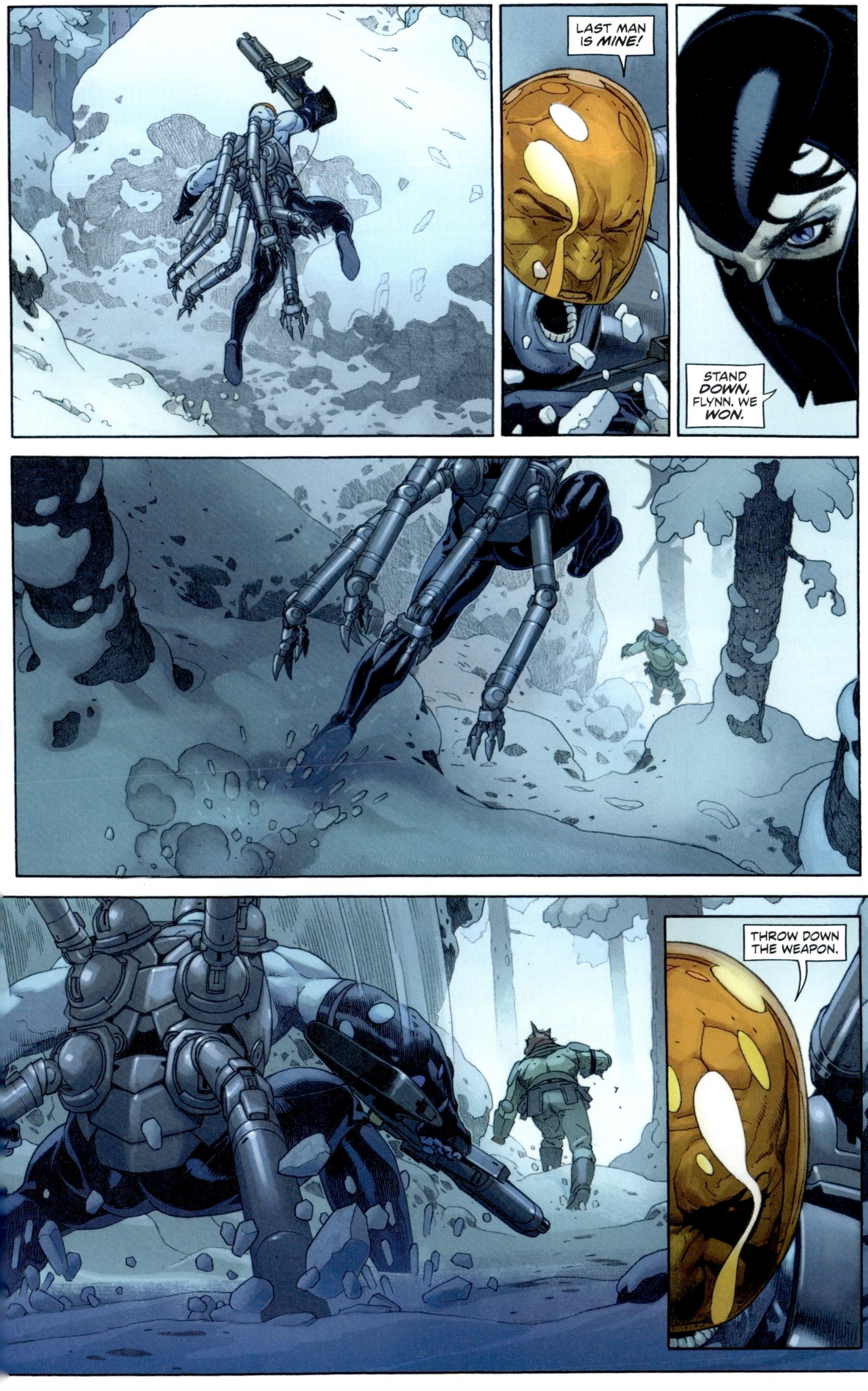
LAST MAN IS MINE!
STAND DOWN, FLYNN. WE WON.
THROW DOWN THE WEAPON.

SOMEBODY CALL IT. *NOW* WE'RE--
HOLO-DRONE.
THAT IS A *CLASSIC*.
OLD MAN, YOU SHOULDA STAYED ASLEEP.
BZZZZATT

DEVI! WHAT WAS GOING THROUGH YOUR MIND OUT THERE?
I'VE GOT A GOOD TEAM. AND WE'VE ALL GOT FAMILY HOME THAT KEEP US STRONG OUT THERE.
SHE'S GOOD.
TO FOCUS GROUPS SHE'S TOO GOOD. THEY WANT TO SEE THE SEAMS.
WE RISE TOMORROW, HELD UP BY ALL OF YOU.
CAN WE TURN THAT OFF?!
THIS IS WHAT I DO, FLYNN. I'M YOUR PUBLICIST. I'M GOING TO FLIP YOUR DAY AROUND.
THAT LOSS IS GOING TO TANK THE UNDERWRITERS. THEIR BANK'S GONNA CRUMBLE. I JUST SENT THOUSANDS OF PEOPLE HOME FROM WORK.
WE BOTH KNOW THIS IS DONE.

FEELIN' ALRIGHT, FLYNN? THEY COOKED YOUR BRAIN UP PRETTY GOOD FROM WHAT I SAW.
THEY SHOULDA COOKED IT MORE.
I CAN'T TALK RIGHT NOW, I'M WITH A CLIENT.
ARE YOU IN A BLENDER? I CAN BARELY HEAR YOU. I'M GOING INTO THE HALL.
AT LEAST THEY DIDN'T GET THE LEG.
I'M SORRY, FLYNN.
YOU LOST YOUR SPONSOR.

YOU WON'T BELIEVE A WORD OF THIS, FLYNN. NOT A SINGLE WORD.
I DON'T WANNA HEAR A SINGLE WORD. JUST WANNA GO HOME AND SLEEP AND MAYBE NEVER WAKE UP.
YOU DON'T UNDERSTAND ME, YOU'VE GOTTA LOOK AT THIS...
CAN SOMEONE TURN ON THE VID?!
SOMETHING HAPPENED, FLYNN! THE SKY LIT UP FOR YOU.
YOUR RATINGS, FLYNN...YOUR RATINGS...
...THEY'RE THROUGH THE ROOF!
LIEUTENANT FLYNN
WEEKLY RATINGS ARC
[ALL DEMOGRAPHICS]
Brought to you by
CHERRY COMBAT
MORE TO COME!
We'll be back after these messages.

COMMERCIAL MESSAGE
PRAYER BOOST
Give your pleas
The priority they deserve
PRAYER BOOST
PRAYER BOOST
PRAYER BOOST

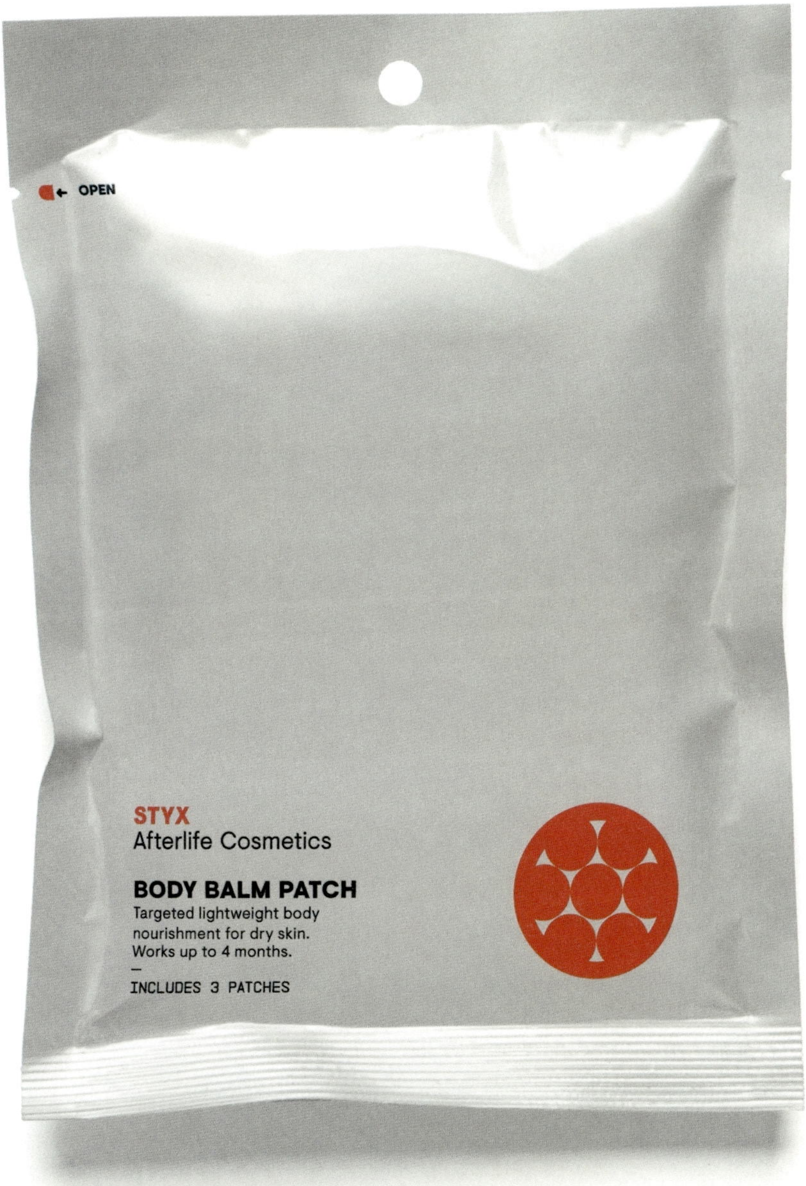
OPEN
STYX
Afterlife Cosmetics
BODY BALM PATCH
Targeted lightweight body
nourishment for dry skin.
Works up to 4 months.
—
INCLUDES 3 PATCHES

LOADING:
TONIGHT'S
WAR
ANNOUNCEMENT
CHAPTER 3

CAN YOU HEAR ME?
CAN HE HEAR ME?
VITTORIO CAN NOT HEAR IN THERE.
HE CAN ONLY SPEAK.
WE HAVE JUST TO LISTEN.

IT IS THE LAST DAY AGAIN.

NOTICE
PLEASE BE CALM.
NOTICE
MAKE CAREFUL WAY FOR THE ASCENDANT.

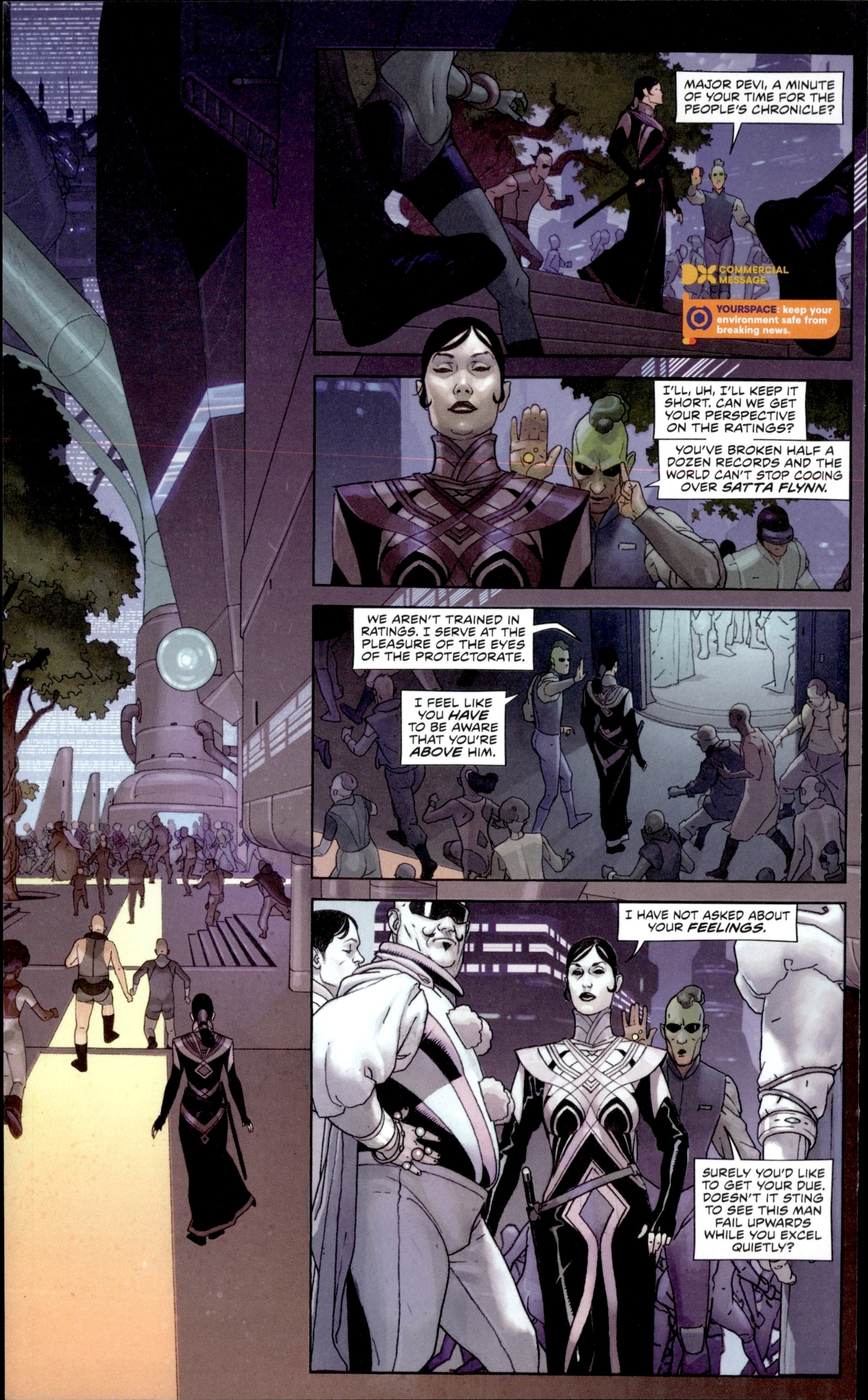

MAJOR DEVI, A MINUTE OF YOUR TIME FOR THE PEOPLE'S CHRONICLE?
DX COMMERCIAL MESSAGE
YOURSPACE: keep your environment safe from breaking news.
I'LL, UH, I'LL KEEP IT SHORT. CAN WE GET YOUR PERSPECTIVE ON THE RATINGS?
YOU'VE BROKEN HALF A DOZEN RECORDS AND THE WORLD CAN'T STOP COOING OVER SATTA FLYNN.
WE AREN'T TRAINED IN RATINGS. I SERVE AT THE PLEASURE OF THE EYES OF THE PROTECTORATE.
I FEEL LIKE YOU HAVE TO BE AWARE THAT YOU'RE ABOVE HIM.
I HAVE NOT ASKED ABOUT YOUR FEELINGS.
SURELY YOU'D LIKE TO GET YOUR DUE. DOESN'T IT STING TO SEE THIS MAN FAIL UPWARDS WHILE YOU EXCEL QUIETLY?

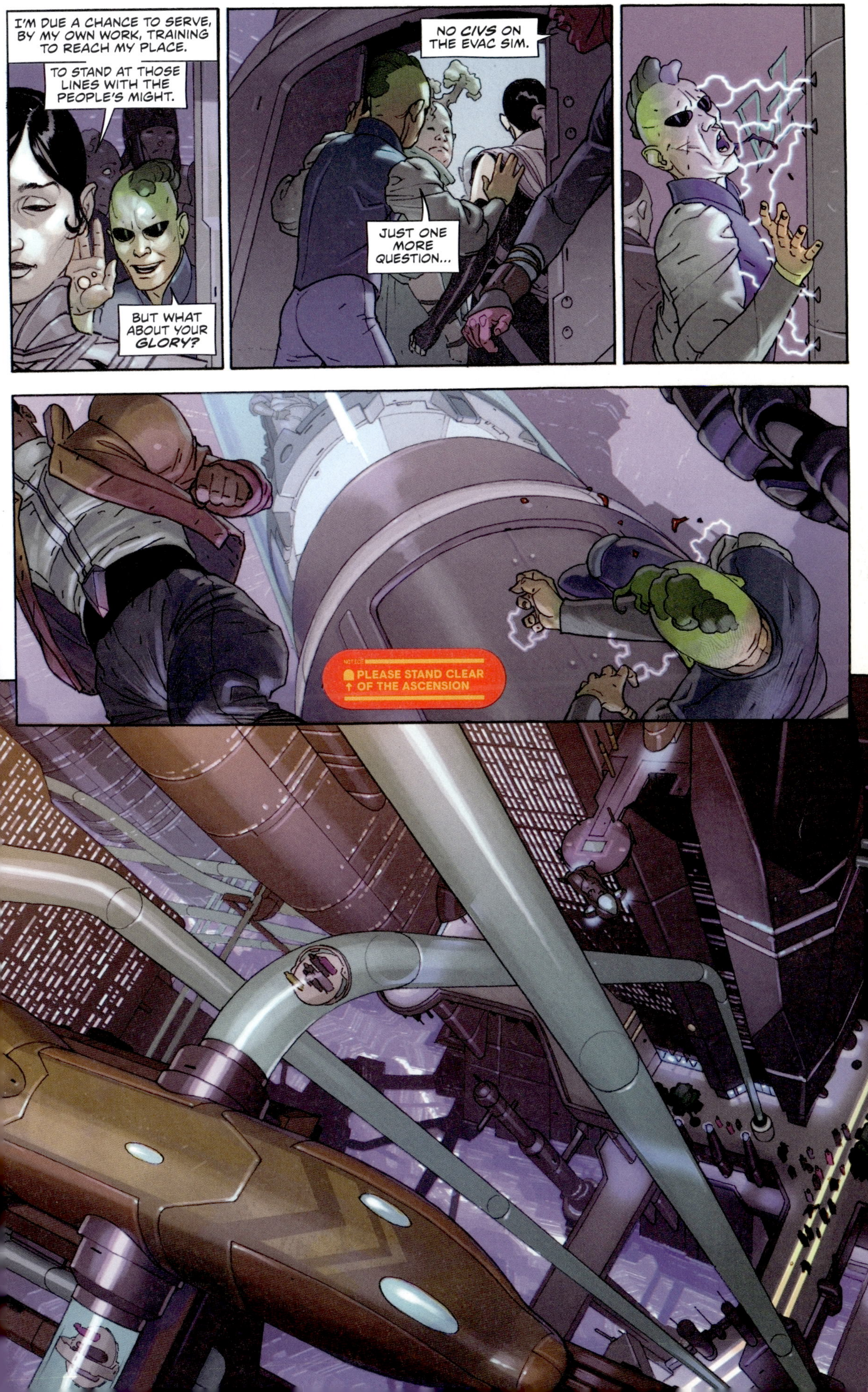
I'M DUE A CHANCE TO SERVE, BY MY OWN WORK, TRAINING TO REACH MY PLACE.
TO STAND AT THOSE LINES WITH THE PEOPLE'S MIGHT.
BUT WHAT ABOUT YOUR *GLORY?*
NO *CIVS* ON THE EVAC SIM.
JUST ONE MORE QUESTION...
PLEASE STAND CLEAR OF THE ASCENSION

WE NEED THE NUMBERS RETABULATED. THIS IS AN ERROR, AND SOMEONE NEEDS TO LOSE THEIR HANDS FOR IT.
THEY'VE BEEN RECOUNTED HALF A BILLION TIMES. THE CODE WE USE FOR POLLING IS A CLOSE SECOND TO WHAT WE USE IN THE ORBITAL...
WE WILL NOT HEAR YOU BLASPHEME IN THIS ROOM!
SOMEONE, NOT ALL OF YOU...
...TELL US HOW WE GOT HERE.

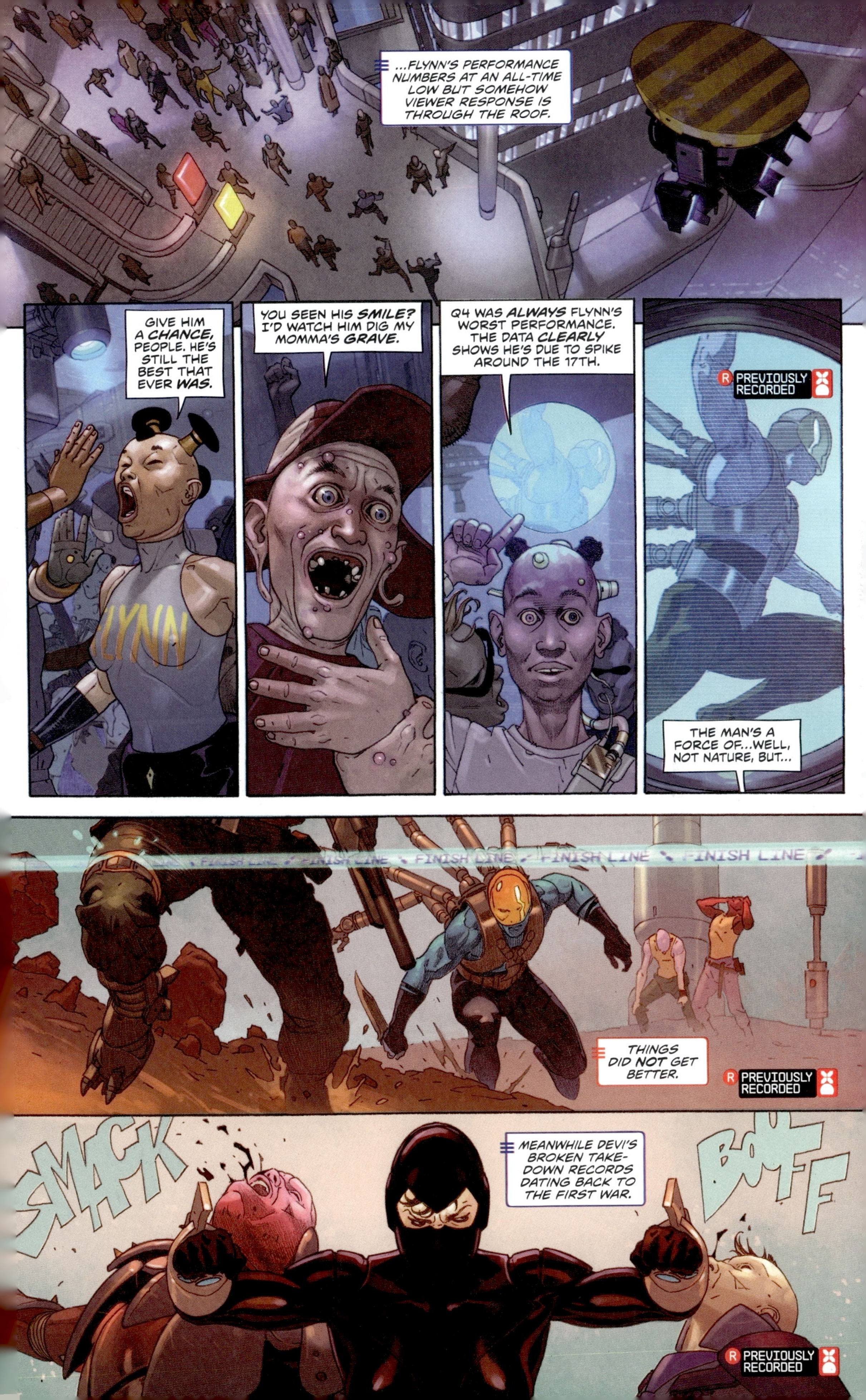
...FLYNN'S PERFORMANCE NUMBERS AT AN ALL-TIME LOW BUT SOMEHOW VIEWER RESPONSE IS THROUGH THE ROOF.
GIVE HIM A CHANCE, PEOPLE. HE'S STILL THE BEST THAT EVER WAS.
FLYNN
YOU SEEN HIS SMILE? I'D WATCH HIM DIG MY MOMMA'S GRAVE.
Q4 WAS ALWAYS FLYNN'S WORST PERFORMANCE. THE DATA CLEARLY SHOWS HE'S DUE TO SPIKE AROUND THE 17TH.
PREVIOUSLY RECORDED
THE MAN'S A FORCE OF...WELL, NOT NATURE, BUT...
FINISH LINE
THINGS DID NOT GET BETTER.
PREVIOUSLY RECORDED
SMACK
BOOFF
MEANWHILE DEVI'S BROKEN TAKE-DOWN RECORDS DATING BACK TO THE FIRST WAR.
PREVIOUSLY RECORDED

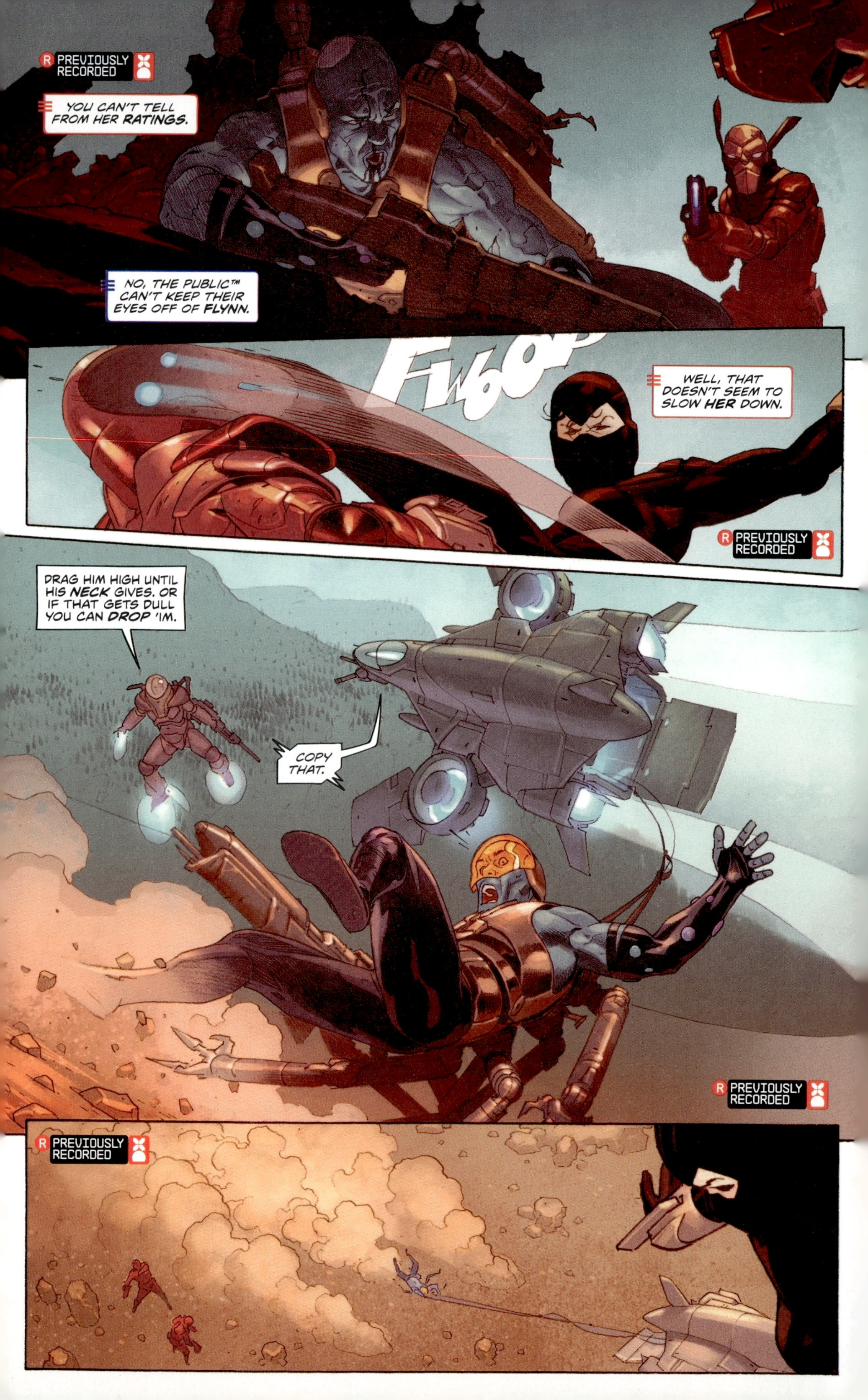
PREVIOUSLY RECORDED
YOU CAN'T TELL FROM HER RATINGS.
NO, THE PUBLIC™ CAN'T KEEP THEIR EYES OFF OF FLYNN.
FWOOP
WELL, THAT DOESN'T SEEM TO SLOW HER DOWN.
PREVIOUSLY RECORDED
DRAG HIM HIGH UNTIL HIS NECK GIVES. OR IF THAT GETS DULL YOU CAN DROP 'IM.
COPY THAT.
PREVIOUSLY RECORDED
PREVIOUSLY RECORDED

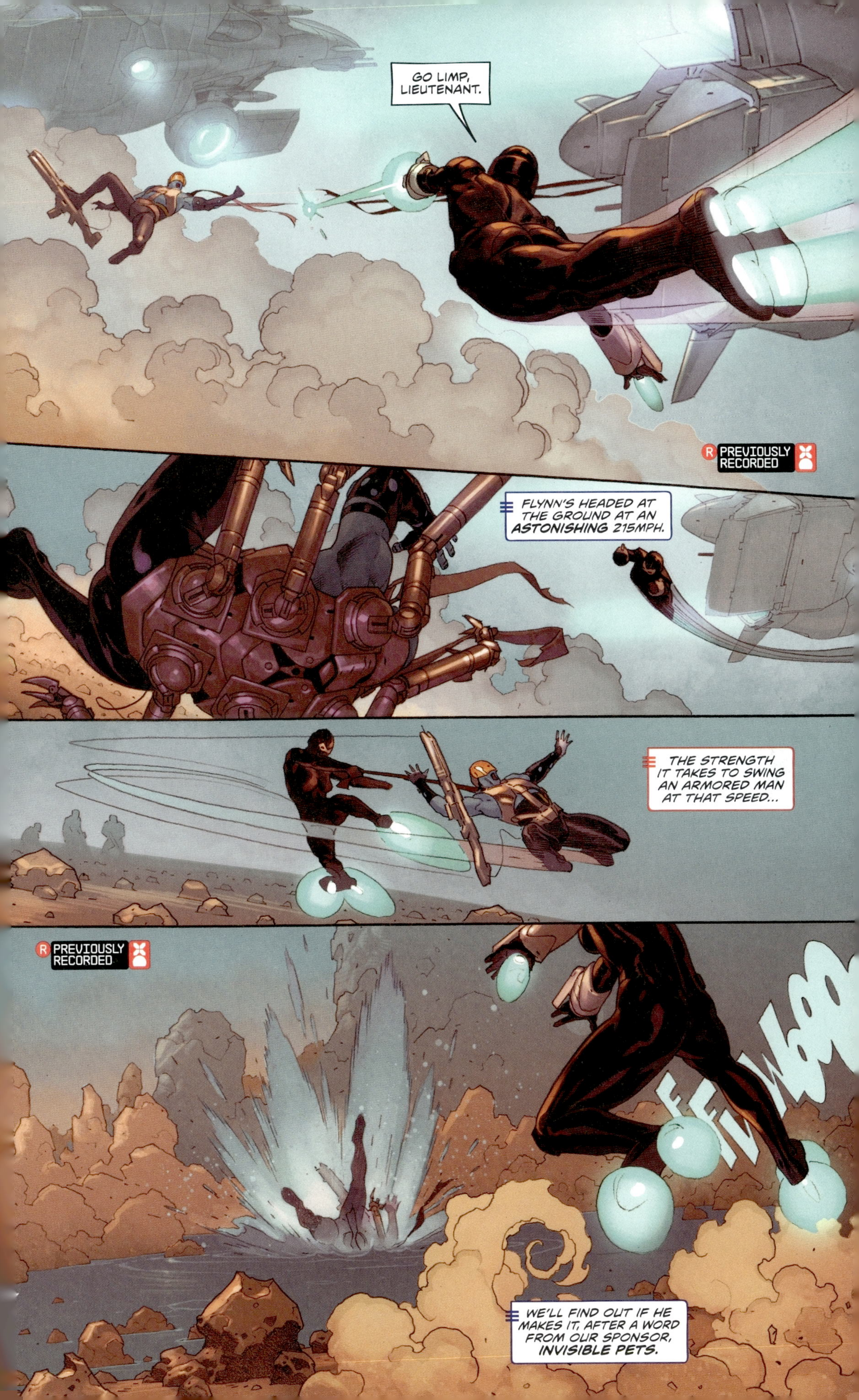

GO LIMP, LIEUTENANT.
PREVIOUSLY RECORDED
FLYNN'S HEADED AT THE GROUND AT AN **ASTONISHING** 215MPH.
THE STRENGTH IT TAKES TO SWING AN ARMORED MAN AT THAT SPEED...
PREVIOUSLY RECORDED
FFWOOO
WE'LL FIND OUT IF HE MAKES IT, AFTER A WORD FROM OUR SPONSOR, **INVISIBLE PETS.**

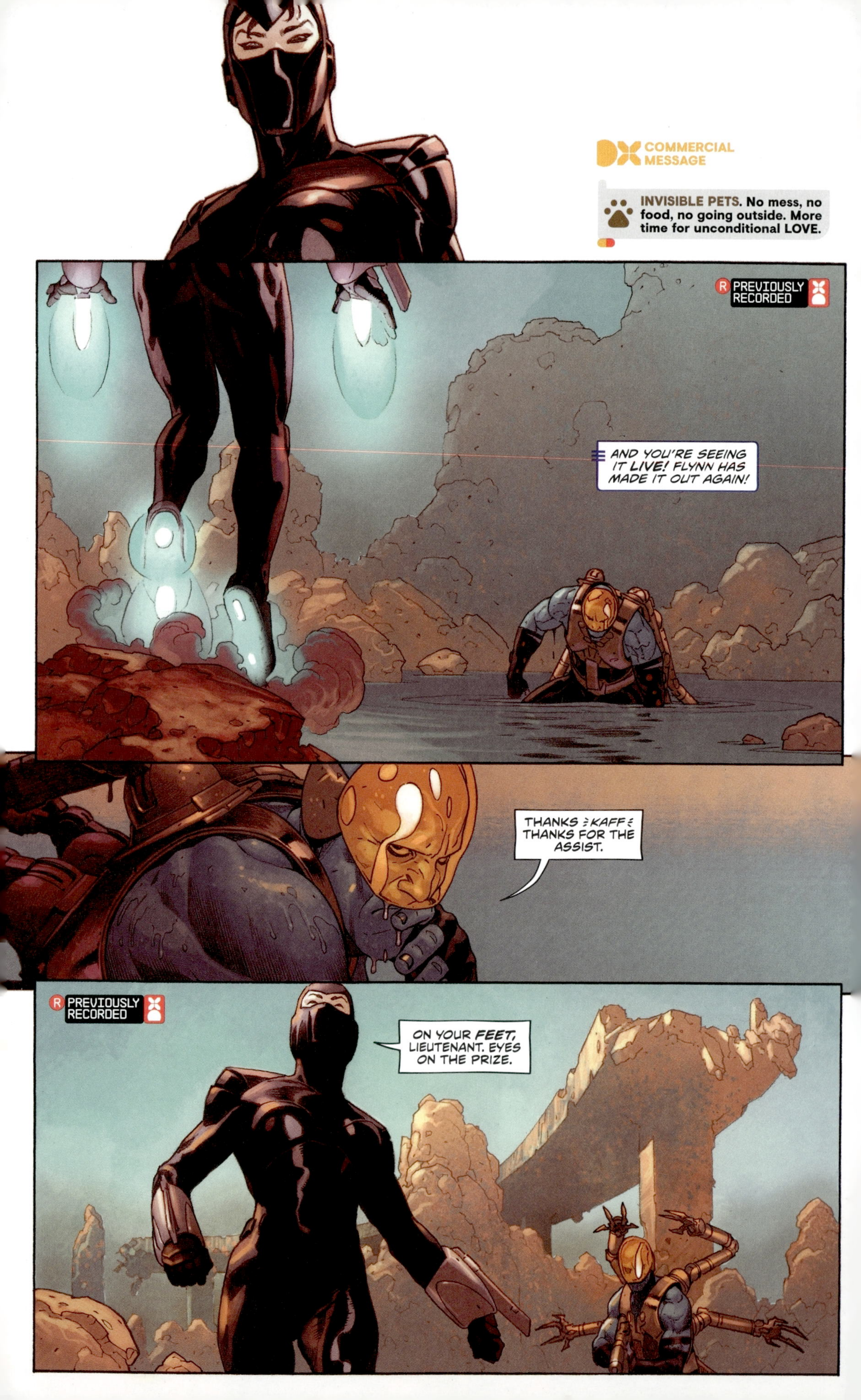
DX COMMERCIAL MESSAGE
INVISIBLE PETS. No mess, no food, no going outside. More time for unconditional LOVE.
PREVIOUSLY RECORDED
AND YOU'RE SEEING IT LIVE! FLYNN HAS MADE IT OUT AGAIN!
THANKS *KAFF* THANKS FOR THE ASSIST.
PREVIOUSLY RECORDED
ON YOUR FEET, LIEUTENANT. EYES ON THE PRIZE.

I'M NOT EXACTLY SURE HOW YOU MANAGED...ALL OF THOSE WORDS.
WE UNDERSTAND IT LESS NOW.
IT'S NOT ENTIRELY CLEAR TO...WE'VE LOOKED A NUMBER OF DIFFERENT WAYS.
THERE IS NO MODEL THAT PREDICTS WHAT WE'RE SEEING. IT IS...
DON'T SAY IMPOSSIBLE. IT IS CLEARLY NOT IMPOSSIBLE.
I LET YOU SPEAK. WILL YOU TALK OVER ME?
IF YOU STOP TALKING, WE CAN SKIP THAT STEP.
WE NEED TO RUN MORE TESTS.
WE...WHAT?
OH THIS IS GREAT.
IT'S...THE ONLY WAY.
SIR, WE CAN'T SAY WITHOUT...
HOW MANY MORE TESTS?
SEE WHAT WE HAVE, AND...

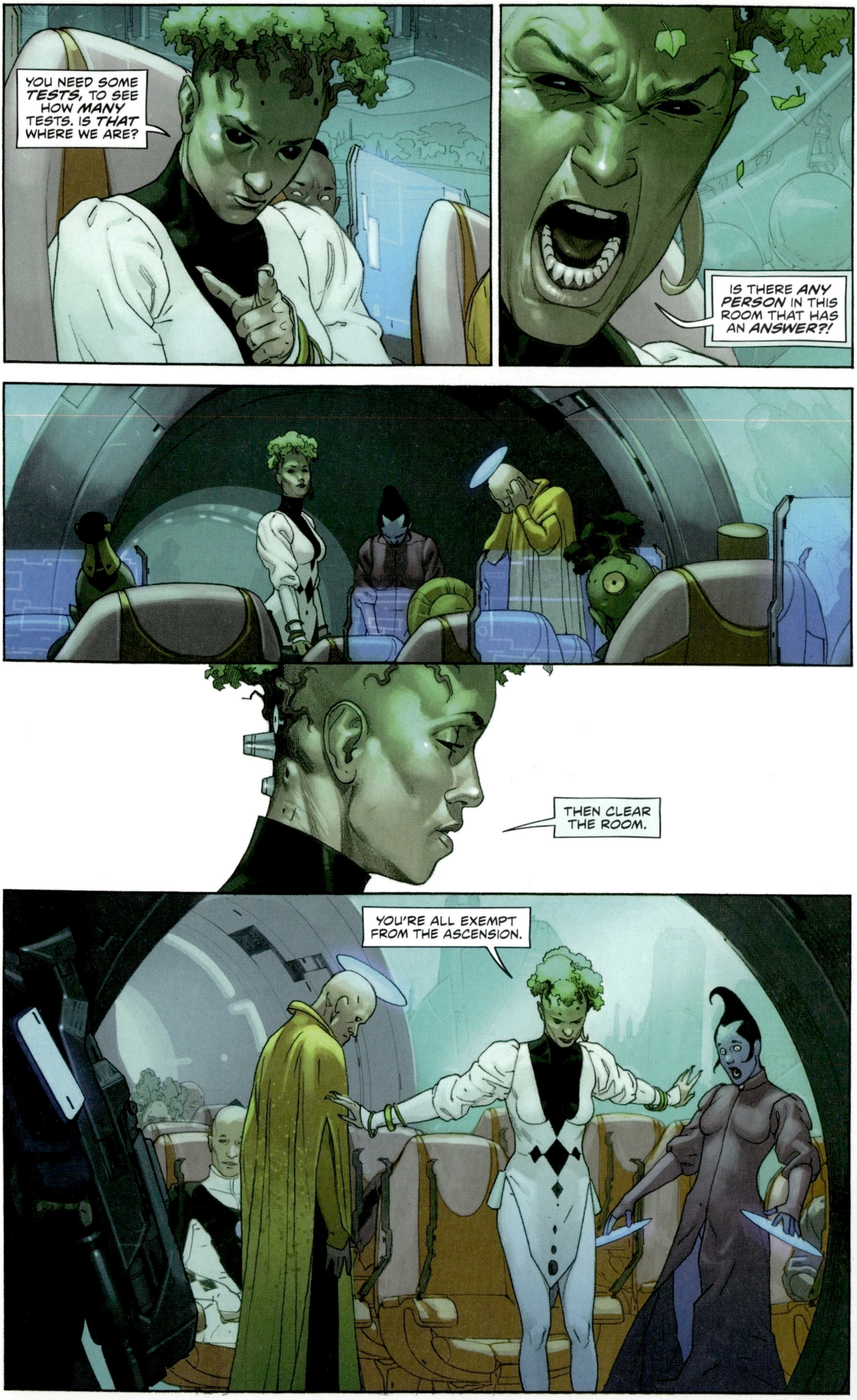
YOU NEED SOME TESTS, TO SEE HOW MANY TESTS. IS THAT WHERE WE ARE?
IS THERE ANY PERSON IN THIS ROOM THAT HAS AN ANSWER?!
THEN CLEAR THE ROOM.
YOU'RE ALL EXEMPT FROM THE ASCENSION.

THIS BOARD IS DISSOLVED. SEND THEM ALL BACK.
NOTICE
WALK SLOWLY. WE ALL RISE TOGETHER.
I WANT A NEW V.P. WITH A TANGIBLE SOLUTION BY THE TIME WE REACH THE HIGHER PLANE.
MUST WE START OVER, ONE?
IT ALWAYS WORKS OUT, TWO.

NOTICE
PLEASE CONSERVE YOUR AIR
NOTICE
THIS IS THE LAST DAY.
NOTICE
IT HAPPENS FAST.

NOTICE
YOU WILL FEEL LIGHT

PLEASE BE MINDFUL OF THE GRAVITY
MAJOR?
I JUST WANTED TO, UH, WANTED TO GIVE YOU MY...
NO.
WHATEVER'S IN YOUR HEAD WIPE IT *OUT.*
LOOK IN MY EYES. MAKE SURE YOU REALLY *HEAR* THIS.
I WORKED A DOZEN YEARS TO GET HERE. MY MOTHER SERVED JUST LIKE *HERS* DID.
MY *EVERY BREATH* IS TRAINING.
THERE IS *NOTHING* THAT YOU GIVE ME.
AND EVEN LESS THAT YOU CAN *TAKE.* I *BUILT* MY LIFE AND IF YOU BOW YOUR HEAD TO PATRONIZE ME YOU'LL NEED A NEW *JAW* TO MATCH THAT *LEG.*
EYES ON THE *JOB,* LIEUTENANT.

WE DON'T HAVE THE LUXURY OF PLEASANTRY, SO DON'T EXPECT INDULGENCE.
THESE LOSSES AREN'T ABOUT PUBLICITY. THE NET LOSS OR GAIN OF WHERE WE STAND IS AT THE BOTTOM OF THE LIST OF WHAT WE'RE HERE FOR. WE HAVE LOST LAND IN THESE BATTLES. AIR RIGHTS. MINING.
WE ARE ENTRUSTED TO PROTECT WHAT'S OURS. TO GROW OUR MEANS. WE CANNOT LOSE, OR THE PROTECTORATE LOSES.
SATTA FLYNN HAS UNSEEN POPULARITY. YOU'RE HERE TO TELL US HOW TO END THAT.
YOUR PREDECESSORS FAILED TO SOLVE THIS IN A WEEK. LEAVING YOU TO SOLVE THIS, NOW. RIGHT IN THIS MOMENT.
WAIT, NOW... ARE YOU...ARE YOU EATING?

I DIDN'T EAT ALL DAY. AND THEN THE EVAC HIT LIKE...RIGHT OUTSIDE THE LUNCHROOM. LIKE--PAINFULLY CLOSE.
WHO BROUGHT THIS...PERSON IN HERE? TELL ME YOUR NAME SO YOU CAN JOIN HIM WHEN WE FLUSH HIM INTO ORBIT.
WELL, I'M NOT MUCH FOR BUREAUCRATS IN ANY CASE.
NO DISRESPECT. I WANTED SOMETHING ON THE FIELD.
WHY IS HE STILL HERE?
DAMN SHAME SHE SAVED HIM. IF HE'DA DIED YOU GROSS OLD MONSTERS COULDA FLOWN HIM UP TO HEAVEN ON A HERO'S RATINGS.
MOVE FAST TO LEAVE AND SHUT YOUR MOUTH.
NO, WAIT!

TELL US AGAIN, PLEASE. GIVE HIM A SEAT.
DO...WHAT?
PREVIOUSLY RECORDED
"TELL US ABOUT THE DEATH OF SATTA FLYNN."
STAY WHERE YOU ARE!
There's more to come!

COMMERCIAL
MESSAGE

DERMAZAN™

Side effects may include grumpiness

INTRODUCING THE BIOSHIELD
HOMESEC™ CENTURION B*

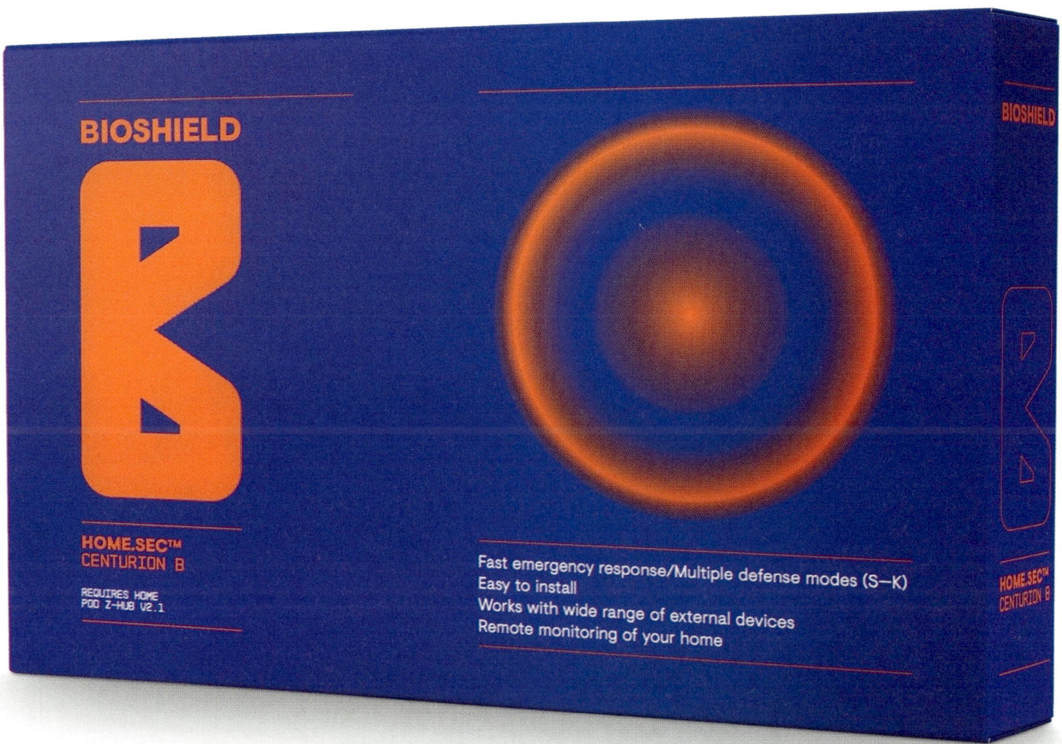

*REQUIRES HOME POD Z-HUB V2.1

BIOSHIELD

With Bioshield your home is yours again.

Forever.

LOADING: TONIGHT'S WAR
ANNOUNCEMENT
CHAPTER 4

IS THAT *THEM?*
IT'S NOT.
WAIT...
IT *IS!* DO YOU *SEE* HIM?
PRAISE THE OVERSIGHT!
FLYNN!
STAND *BACK*, THERE WILL BE *NO* MORE WARNINGS.
FLYNN!

WAIT!
FLYNN!
NOTICE
VIEWSHIELD IS FOR YOUR OWN PROTECTION.
ARE YOU READY FOR YOUR HOMETOWN DEFENDERS? I CAN'T HEAAAR YOUUUUU...
THIS GEAR DOESN'T FEEL RIGHT. IT'S TOO MUCH.
IT DOESN'T LOOK RIGHT IF EVERY-ONE'S MARCHING INTO GLORY AND YOU'RE IN HERE FUTZING, EITHER.
THIS DOESN'T SUIT ME.
YOU'RE STATE OF THE ART, BABY. BETTER THAN EVER. AND YOU WERE ALREADY THE BEST.

THE PEOPLE ASKED FOR YOU TO STAND FOR THEM. YOU HAVE TO GO OUT THERE AND STAND.
MAKE SOME NOISE FOR HISTORY!

NEW SPONSORS! TOP SECRET GEAR HEAD TO TOE! SATTA FLYNN HAS HAD A WARTIME MAKEOVER!
WHAT'S OLD IS NEW AGAIN!
DX ANNOUNCEMENT
Welcome to the 36th annual CIRCUS IMMANIS

THIS IS DISTURBING.
GAUDY.
HOW MUCH CAN ALL OF THAT HAVE COST? ENOUGH TO FEED THE ENTIRE DISTRICT.
THIS IS THE PLAN. THIS IS THE PLAN. REPEAT UNTIL IT DOESN'T HURT.
HEY NOW, LOOK AT CAPTAIN OUTER SPACE OVER HERE.
MAMA! I THOUGHT YOU WERE TRANS-FERRED.
NAH, JUST DETENTION. I ACCIDENTALLY BEAT UP ALL THE GUARDS.
KINDA EASIER FOR EVERY-ONE IF I'M OUT HERE HITTING THE ENEMY.
PLUS I'M YOUR LUCKY CHARM. I'M HERE TO HELP YOU REMEMBER WHAT KICKING XXXX FEELS LIKE.
FLYNN, INTO THE CAM.
FLYNN, LOOK OVER HERE.
I DO REMEMBER. THAT'S THE PROBLEM.

FOR THE FIRST ROUND, THE WORLD'S BIGGEST ANNUAL WAR EVENT WELCOMES: THE ROAD WIDOWS FROM THE SOUTHERN FLOTILLA.
THE INVISIBLE STATE.
AND THE UNNAMED FROM THE QUIET SEAS.

YOU GOT ORDERS?
I DON'T GIVE ORDERS ANYMORE.
BRAVO TEAM! FAN OUT AND CIRCLE! GO GO GO!
I LEFT YOU WITH GLORY IN YOUR HANDS.
I WON THAT ONE.
STICK WITH ME, FLYNN. I THINK I SAW YOUR GLORY IN THE BUSHES DOWN A WAYS.
EVERY-BODY LOVES THAT SOUND! HERE WE GO!
THIS.
MEANS.
WAR!
SPONSORED BY:
CHERRY COMBAT

TOO CLOSE, MARTINEZ.
ONE MOMENT, PLEASE.
YOU CAN'T EVEN KNOW HOW MUCH I MISSED THIS.
WE'RE DUCKS OUT HERE.
EAGLE EYE ON FLYNN!
DID THEY REPLACE THAT, TOO?

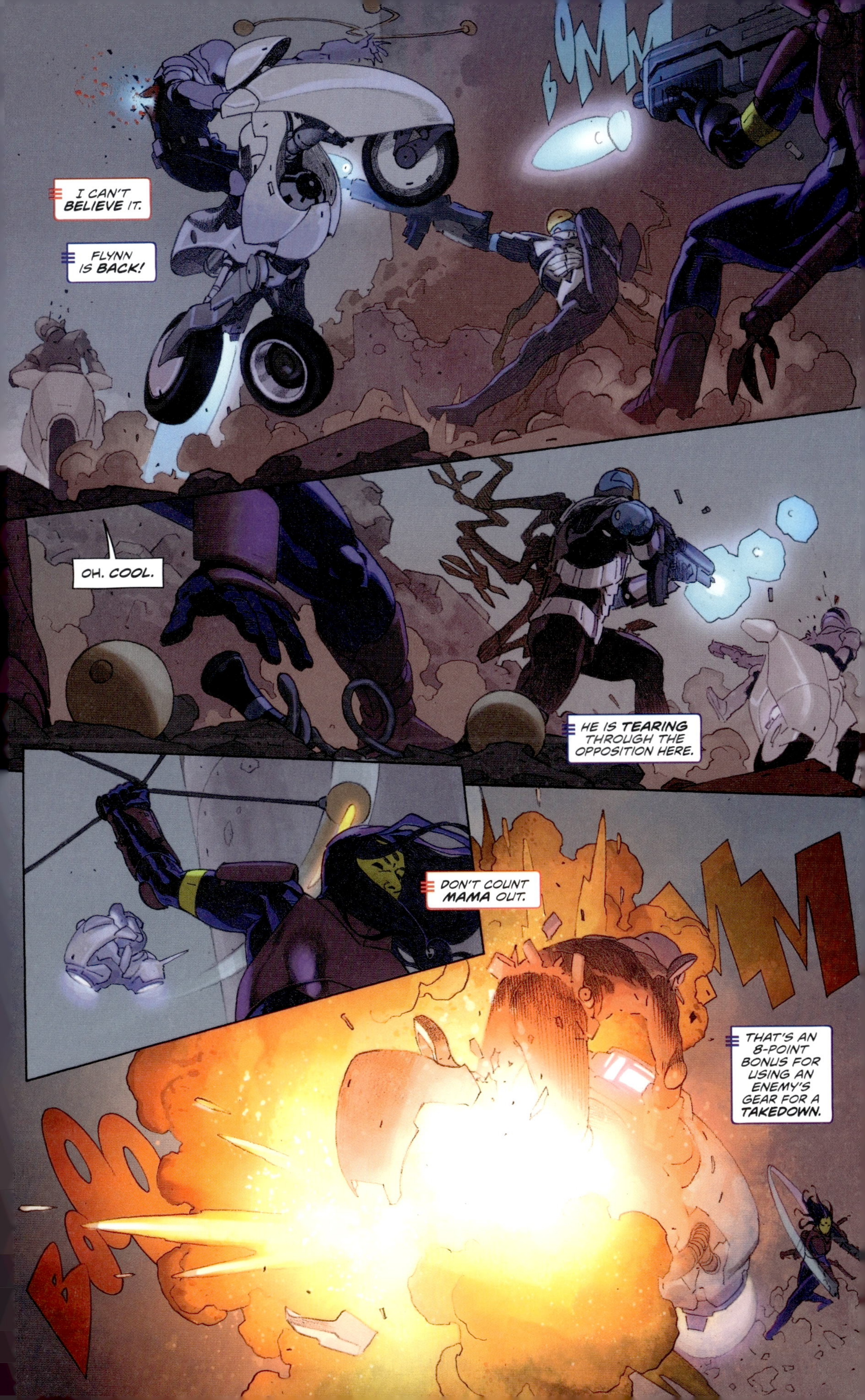
I CAN'T BELIEVE IT.
FLYNN IS BACK!
OH. COOL.
HE IS TEARING THROUGH THE OPPOSITION HERE.
DON'T COUNT MAMA OUT.
THAT'S AN 8-POINT BONUS FOR USING AN ENEMY'S GEAR FOR A TAKEDOWN.

NOW *THAT'S* THE SATTA FLYNN I SWORE I'D VISIT HELL WITH.
RUN ALONG, FRIENDS...YOUR DESSERT'S GETTING COLD.
HEY! WHAT'S THE--*HRRKK*
I--
NO! WAIT! XXXX!
OUCH! RIGHT INTO THE ***THOROUGHFARE!***
WHAT IS ***HAPPENING?!*** *I'M ON THE EDGE OF MY* ***SEAT!***
MOTHERXXXX.

SPLAT
CHIEF, CAN YOU HEAR ME? I NEED PIT ASSIST.
ARM'S HAYWIRE. BLOCK OFF MY LOCATIONNNNNN--
--NNNNNAAAHHHH!!
KSHH
ERROR: MESSAGE NOT DELIVERED_
DID FLYNN JUST RIP HIS OWN ARM OFF?!
WILDEST CIRCUS IMMANIS I'VE EVER SEEN.
CHIEF? DO YOU COPY?
I'M NOT A TACTICAL SPECIALIST, BUT FLYNN PROBABLY NEEDS TO GET OFF THE ROADWAY.
FLYNN!!
KRNNK

DIE, ROBOT CAR!!
BRAAZT
AREN'T THOSE CARS AUTOMATED?
MUST BE A SYSTEM ERROR. WHAT A TURN FOR SATTA FLYNN AFTER A BEAUTIFUL START.
THAT CAR'S STILL MOVING...
GLORY TO THE PEOPLE.
BOOOM

MAMA?
HOLY OVERSIGHT! AND THAT'S OUR--
SAVE OF THE DAY
Brought to you by: MIRRORSTREAMS
COMMERCIAL MESSAGE
Mirrorstreams: every day a new you.
YOUR COM'S STATIC. LOUD STATIC.
WE'RE SEEING A LOT OF TECHNICAL DIFFICULTIES ON THE PROTECTORATE SIDE.
TELL ME WHAT'S HAPPENING.
MAJOR, THESE NEW ARMS, THERE'S SOMETHING...
SNIKK
AHHGG!!
FZZT
I'M SORRY, I DIDN'T...
AT EASE, LIEUTENANT.

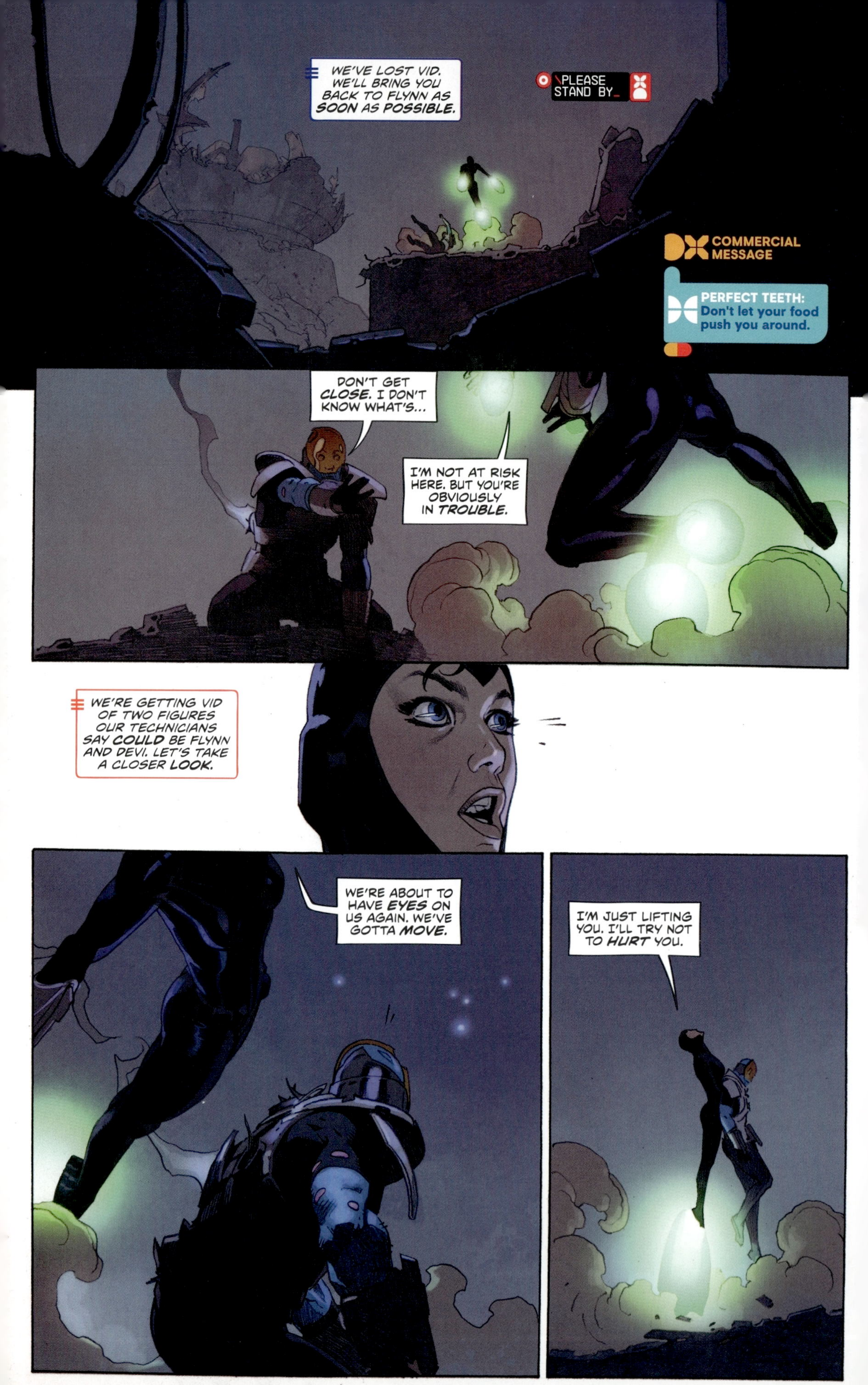

WE'VE LOST VID. WE'LL BRING YOU BACK TO FLYNN AS SOON AS POSSIBLE.
PLEASE STAND BY_
COMMERCIAL MESSAGE
PERFECT TEETH: Don't let your food push you around.
DON'T GET CLOSE. I DON'T KNOW WHAT'S...
I'M NOT AT RISK HERE. BUT YOU'RE OBVIOUSLY IN TROUBLE.
WE'RE GETTING VID OF TWO FIGURES OUR TECHNICIANS SAY COULD BE FLYNN AND DEVI. LET'S TAKE A CLOSER LOOK.
WE'RE ABOUT TO HAVE EYES ON US AGAIN. WE'VE GOTTA MOVE.
I'M JUST LIFTING YOU. I'LL TRY NOT TO HURT YOU.

YOUR TEETH ARE GONNA GRIND A LITTLE.
FWOOOO...
HOLD ONNNNNNN--
WE'VE GOT A GLIMPSE BUT SHE'S MOVING TOO FAST FOR BROADCAST.
PLEASE STAND BY_
OH, GREAT.
FTUM
I THINK WE NEED TO SLOW...

WE'RE GOING LIVE TO FLYNN AND DEVI IN THE JUNKYARD SECTOR.
OOF, THAT PROBABLY HURT.
DEVICE SHUTDOWN. DELTA NINER SEVEN.
SHUT DOWN! DELTA NINER SEVEN!!
GET OUT OF HERE, SUIT'S GLITCHING OUT.
NNNNN
IS SHE...WHY IS SHE AIMING AT FLYNN?
FFOM
I DON'T HAVE CONTROL.
SORRY. FOR ALL OF THIS.
THIS SUIT...WE TRAINED FOR YOU. YOU WERE THE METRIC WHEN WE STARTED.
MY WHOLE GENERATION. TO LIVE UP TO YOU.
WE'RE EXPERIENCING TECHNICAL DIFFICULTIES.

THIS IS NOT THE PLAN.
VERY NOT. I DON'T KNOW WHAT THIS IS.
AND THEN SURPASS WHAT YOU'D DONE. WE GOT PAST YOUR STATS ON VERSION 12. THIS IS VERSION 55.
IF YOU DON'T RUN NOW, THERE WON'T BE A WAY.
I CAN'T... MOVE...
I CAN'T...
KRSHH
OH NO.

THIS ISN'T A MISTAKE.

PERIENCING TECHNICAL DIFFICULTIES_ WE ARE EXPERIENCING TECHNICAL DIFFICULTIES_ WE ARE EXPERIENCING TECHNICAL DIFFICULTIES_
WHAT IS THAT THING?
I DON'T THINK IT'S ME. SOMEBODY WANTS YOU DEAD.
THIS FACTORY LEADS OUTSIDE THE WALLS. OUTSIDE THE PEAK. THE COMS AREN'T WIRED OUT THERE, YOU UNDERSTAND?
NO?
OH, XXXX.
REMEMBER WHAT I SAID. THERE ARE NO COM-WEBS OUTSIDE.

THIS IS NOT WHAT I ASKED FOR!
NO ONE CAN FIND YOU OUT THERE, FLYNN, GOOD OR BAD.
GLORY TO THE PEOPLE.

STAY WHERE YOU ARE!
There's more to come!

MUSIC MILK
Good taste is IN you.
DX COMMERCIAL MESSAGE
STAYS FRESH FOR 16 DAYS
330ML
OPEN

COMMERCIAL
MESSAGE
YOURSPACE
Keep your environment safe from breaking news

LOADING:
TONIGHT'S
WAR
ANNOUNCEMENT
CHAPTER 5

GET IT DONE ALREADY!
BOOOO
WE'LL...WE'LL BE BACK TO THE GAME JUST AS SOON AS...OH MY GOD...
COMMERCIAL MESSAGE
Do you ever feel like the world is on your back? Try SENSORY SHUTDOWN.
WE'RE GETTING A NOTE HERE THAT THE SHOW WILL CONTINUE...IT SAYS "MUST" HERE, IN GIANT LETTERS... AFTER THIS BREAK.

I NEVER MEANT FOR...
IT'S TOO LATE FOR WHAT YOU MEANT. THIS IS WHERE WE ARE.
WE'LL NEED A PARADE. THEY'LL WANT TO MOURN HIM. AND MEMORIAL RATES ARE...
...WE BILL AT TWO AND A HALF TIMES STANDARD PRIMETIME QUOTES.
YOU GUYS ARE REALLY SOMETHING ELSE.

MY MOTHER TALKED ABOUT THE NIGHT SKY. I NEVER *IMAGINED...*
WE HAVE NO TIME FOR REVELRY.
THIS IS A **WILD** NIGHT, BUT YOU CAN SEE THAT SOME OF THESE FIGHTERS ARE **PREOCCUPIED.**
EVERYONE WANTS TO KNOW JUST **WHAT** HAS HAPPENED TO SATTA **FL**
WE'RE NOT SUPPOSED TO MENTION...

MAMA MARTINEZ HAS BEEN ESPECIALLY QUIET ON THE FIELD SINCE...
SINCE EARLIER TONIGHT.
IN NOMINE DOMUS!
YOU GUYS CAN NEVER SHUT YOUR MOUTH.
FZZZZZT
PIT ASSISTANCE! I AM INJURED!
SHE DOESN'T LOOK INJURED.
THIS IS A FIRST, IN SEVEN YEARS MAMA MARTINEZ HAS NEVER LEFT BATTLE FOR AN INJURY. SHE WON THE BATTLE OF THE BRIDGE WITH FOUR BROKEN FINGERS.
YOU DON'T LOOK INJURED.
I COULD BE DYING.

ALRIGHT, I'LL GET YOU UP AND RUN SOME TESTS. YOUR TIMING'S NOT GREAT, MAMA.
THEY REALLY NEED YOU OUT THERE NOW...
HE DIDN'T DO IT. I SAW THE WHOLE THING.
FLYNN? SHIT.
YOU PROBABLY SHOULDN'T HAVE SAID ANYTHING.

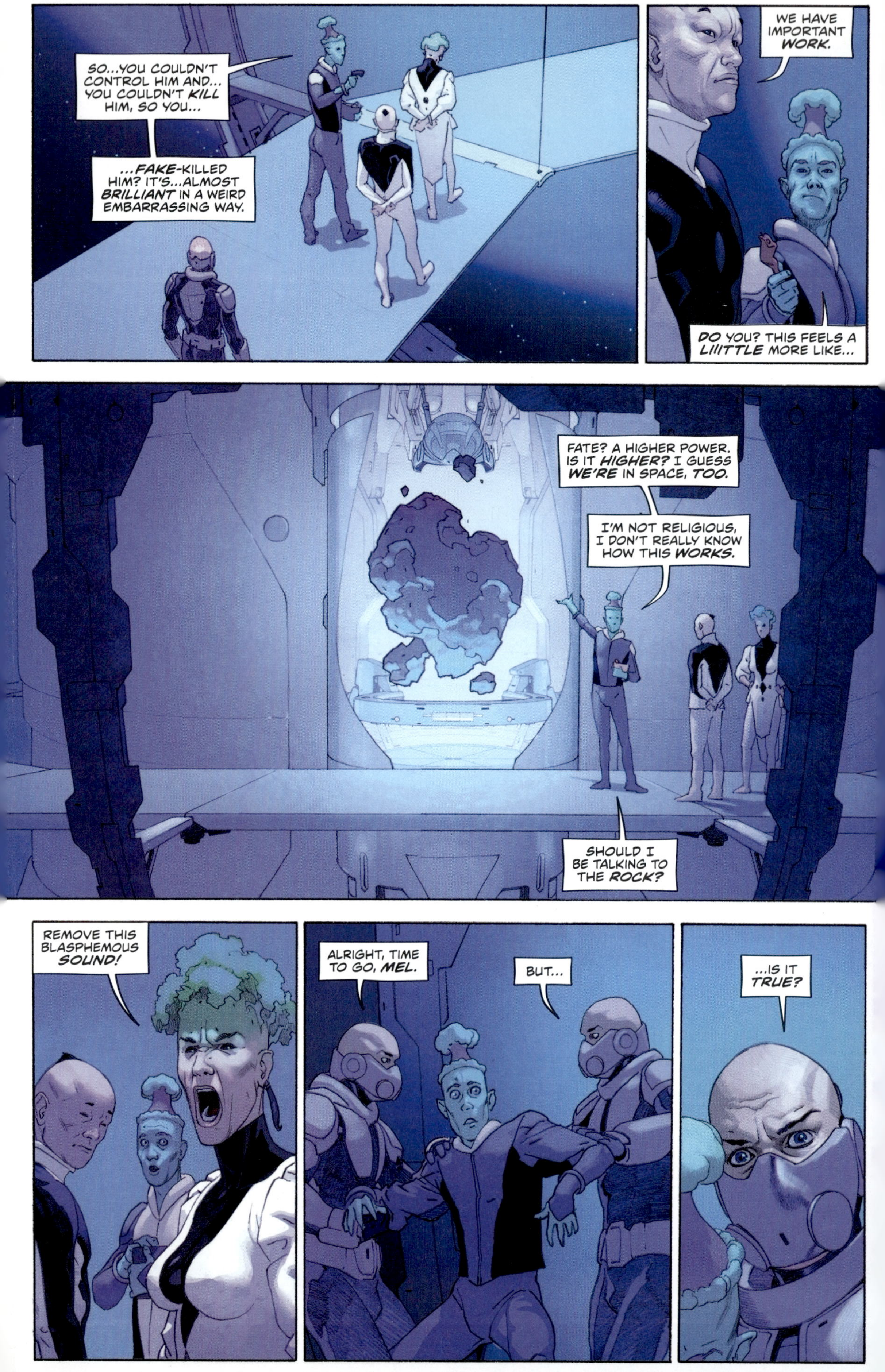
SO...YOU COULDN'T CONTROL HIM AND... YOU COULDN'T KILL HIM, SO YOU...
...FAKE-KILLED HIM? IT'S...ALMOST BRILLIANT IN A WEIRD EMBARRASSING WAY.
WE HAVE IMPORTANT WORK.
DO YOU? THIS FEELS A LIIITTLE MORE LIKE...
FATE? A HIGHER POWER. IS IT HIGHER? I GUESS WE'RE IN SPACE, TOO.
I'M NOT RELIGIOUS, I DON'T REALLY KNOW HOW THIS WORKS.
SHOULD I BE TALKING TO THE ROCK?
REMOVE THIS BLASPHEMOUS SOUND!
ALRIGHT, TIME TO GO, MEL.
BUT...
...IS IT TRUE?

SORRY!
IT'S A SCRAMBLER. SO NO ONE CAN HEAR OUTSIDE THIS ROOM. I CALL IT A BRAINSTORM. IT PROTECTS MY IDEAS FROM THEFT.
PAST A FEW MONTHS YOU GET USED TO IT.
I CAN TASTE MY BREAKFAST IN MY THROAT.
ANYWAY, YEAH. I KNOW FLYNN DIDN'T DO IT.
HIS ATTACK CLOCKED FASTER. THE NEWER TECH HAS OUTSIDE RELAYS, TO...WELL, AUGMENT A GRUNT'S MOVES IN A FIGHT. THAT'S WHAT THEY'RE SUPPOSED TO BE FOR ANYWAY.
BUT WHAT WE SAW OUT THERE WASN'T AN ENHANCEMENT. SOMEBODY TOOK THE WHEEL. HE WASN'T IN CONTROL.
JUST TELL ME WHAT TO HIT.
YEAH... THAT'S THE TRICKY PART.
YOU LOOK LIKE SPOILED GARBAGE.
WITH THE BUSTED TECH THE NEW LEG IS MORE A BURDEN THAN AN AID. IT'S HEAVY AND IT'S DRAGGING.
I CAN BLAST IT OFF IF IT'S BUGGING YOU.

NO! SORRY I SAID ANYTHING! I'D RATHER HOBBLE THAN HOP.
WELL, IF IT GETS A MIND OF ITS OWN IT'S GOING THE WAY OF THOSE EXTRA ARMS.
Y'KNOW, YOUR SUIT STOPPED GLITCHING WHEN WE GOT OUTSIDE THE CITY. THAT CRAZY ROBOT FELL APART.
MAYBE IT'S LIKE YOU SAID, NO ONE CAN HEAR US. THE CAMERAS ARE GONE. AND SO IS WHATEVER WAS MESSING WITH US.
IS THAT WHAT YOUR LITTLE VIDEO IS? IT CAN'T SEE THEM ANYMORE, RIGHT? THE ALMIGHTY OVERSIGHT IS BLIND OUT THERE.
THIS IS A GREAT WAR, THE WAR THE LAST TEN CYCLES ALL WERE LEADING TO.
EVERY MINUTE FLYNN'S OUT THERE LOSING SINKS OUR PROTECTORATE DEEPER IN THE MUD.
DO AS SHE SAYS. THE WAR MUST GO ON.
BUT DID...DID YOUR EMINENCES TRY TO KILL SATTA FLYNN?

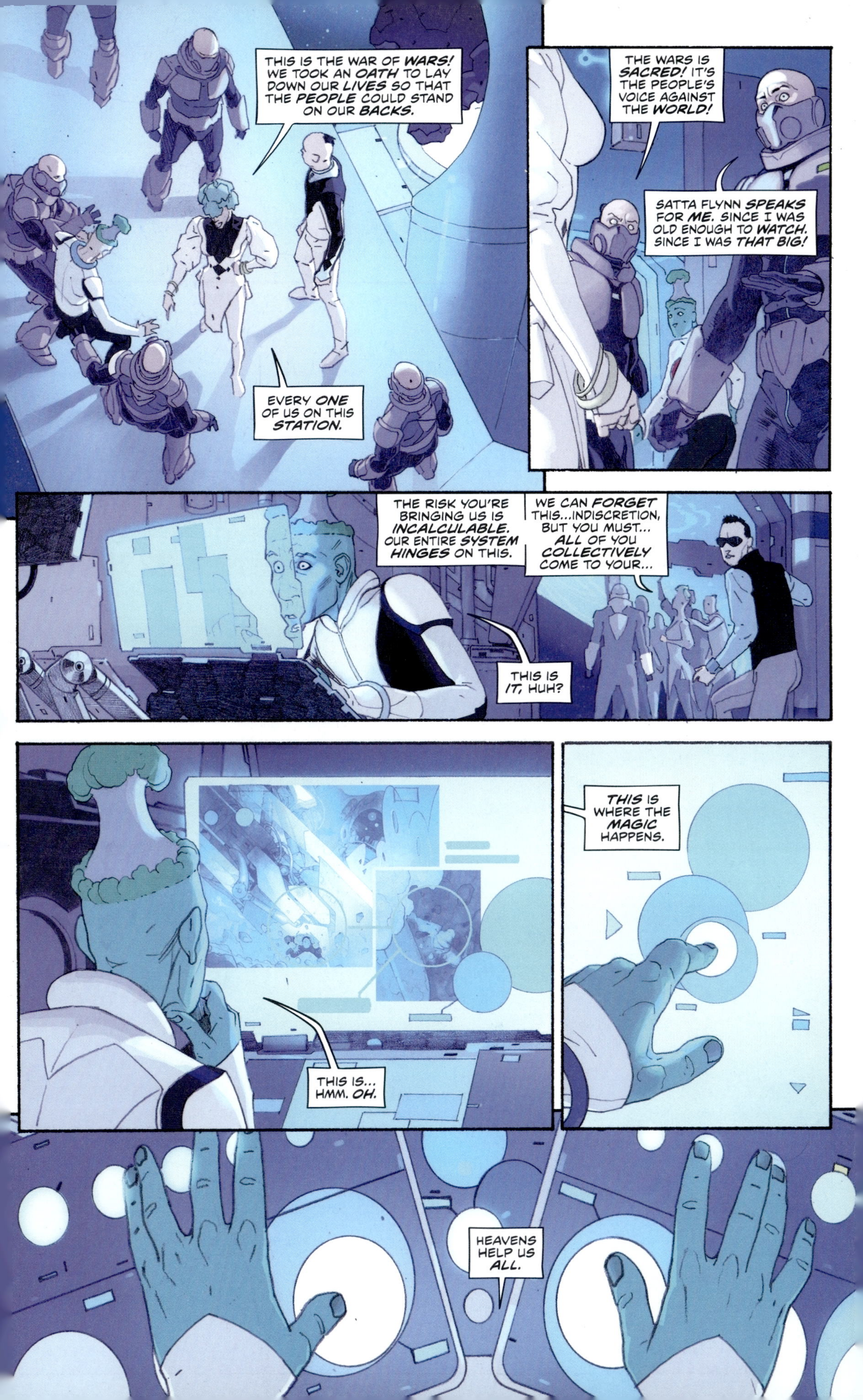
THIS IS THE WAR OF WARS! WE TOOK AN OATH TO LAY DOWN OUR LIVES SO THAT THE PEOPLE COULD STAND ON OUR BACKS.
EVERY ONE OF US ON THIS STATION.
THE WARS IS SACRED! IT'S THE PEOPLE'S VOICE AGAINST THE WORLD!
SATTA FLYNN SPEAKS FOR ME. SINCE I WAS OLD ENOUGH TO WATCH. SINCE I WAS THAT BIG!
THE RISK YOU'RE BRINGING US IS INCALCULABLE. OUR ENTIRE SYSTEM HINGES ON THIS.
WE CAN FORGET THIS...INDISCRETION, BUT YOU MUST... ALL OF YOU COLLECTIVELY COME TO YOUR...
THIS IS IT, HUH?
THIS IS... HMM. OH.
THIS IS WHERE THE MAGIC HAPPENS.
HEAVENS HELP US ALL.

INFO MESSAGE
Due to ongoing practical concerns, the almighty Oversight has sent forth a Holy Stone from above as a corrective measure.
The Stone will circle the planet once and then touch down just outside the walls of The Protectorate.
The impact will bring a new era to our favorite pastime:
WAR!
It will retire Lieutenant Satta Flynn from battle giving him a well-earned and permanent rest.
It is our feeling that The Protectorate's walls were built high enough that it might not kill everyone in the city.
In any case you have a full revolution to enjoy the end of tonight's glorious war event.
Thanks for watching!

FLYNN'S ALIVE?
NOT FOR LONG, SOUNDS LIKE.
WHAT'SAT MEAN? WHAT'SEY SAYING? THEY TRY'NA KILL FLYNN?
THE WARS ARE RIGGED?
WELL, WE SEEM TO BE EXPERIENCING AN...
WE'LL...GET BACK TO THE CIRCUS IMMANIS AS SOON AS WE HAVE WORD FROM...ON HIGH...
I'M NOT DEAD YET. I NEED TO GET BACK IN THERE.
YOU GO BACK YOU'LL BE DEAD SOON ENOUGH.
YOU HAVE TO KNOW WHEN YOU'RE DONE, FLYNN.
THERE'S NO SHAME IN GETTING TO THE END.
THIS IS NOT THE END FOR US, MAJOR, OUT HERE.
THERE'S STILL A FIELD IN THERE. THERE'S STILL A BATTLE.
IF FLYNN'S STILL DOWN THERE, WE CAN SAVE HIM, RIGHT?
I...DON'T THINK ANYONE CAN SAVE FLYNN NOW.

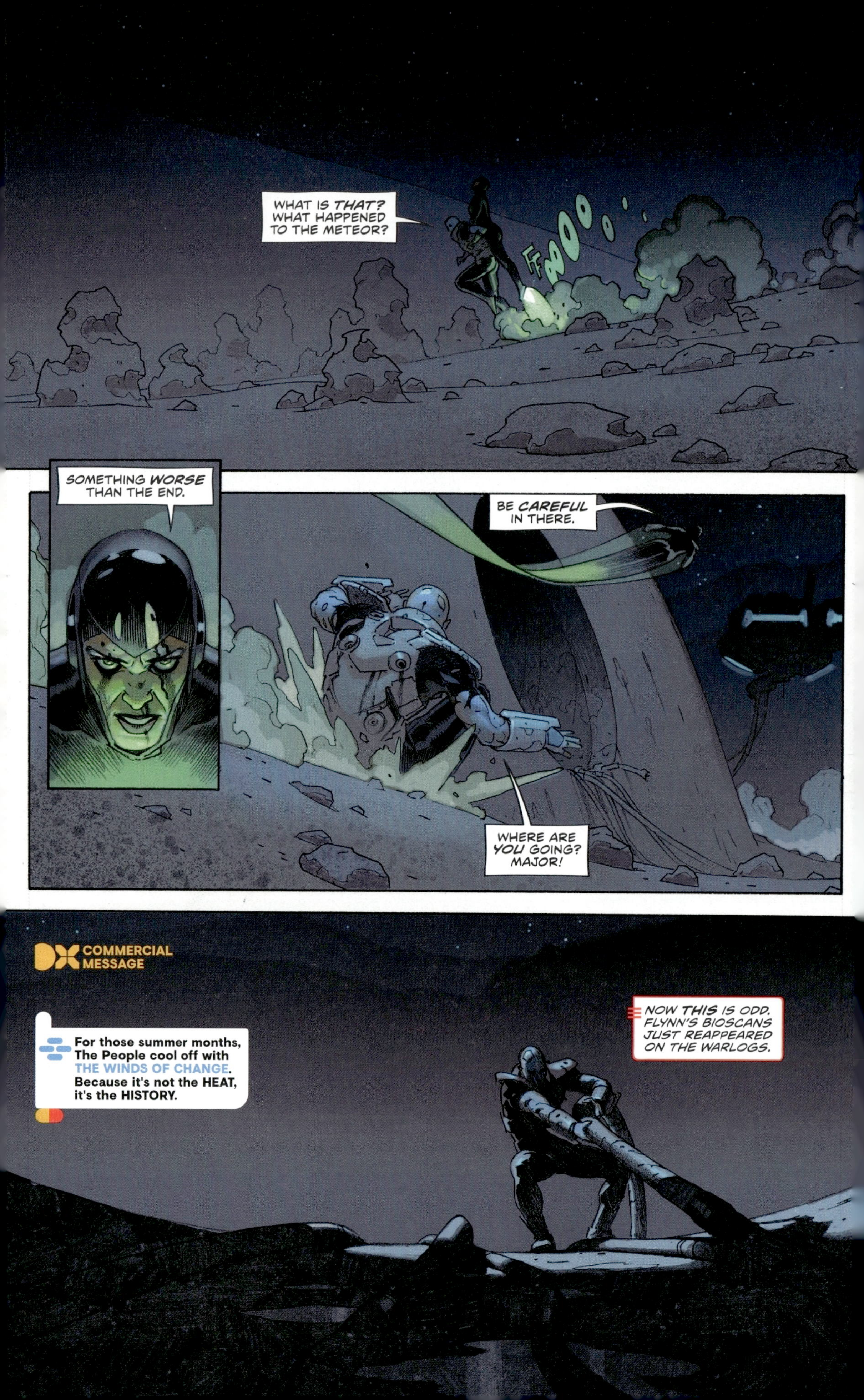
WHAT IS THAT? WHAT HAPPENED TO THE METEOR?
FFWOOOO
SOMETHING WORSE THAN THE END.
BE CAREFUL IN THERE.
WHERE ARE YOU GOING? MAJOR!
DX COMMERCIAL MESSAGE
For those summer months, The People cool off with THE WINDS OF CHANGE. Because it's not the HEAT, it's the HISTORY.
NOW THIS IS ODD. FLYNN'S BIOSCANS JUST REAPPEARED ON THE WARLOGS.

Y'EVER WANNA TRY SOME OF THAT DEATH METAL?
NOT REALLY. I LIKE PUNCHING. I'M A PUNCHER.
IT IS YOUR FINEST QUALITY.
BUT THIS THING WE GOTTA DO... IT COULD PROB'LY USE SOME BIGGER HANDS.
I CAN'T EVEN SAY HOW GLAD I AM TO HEAR YOUR VOICES.

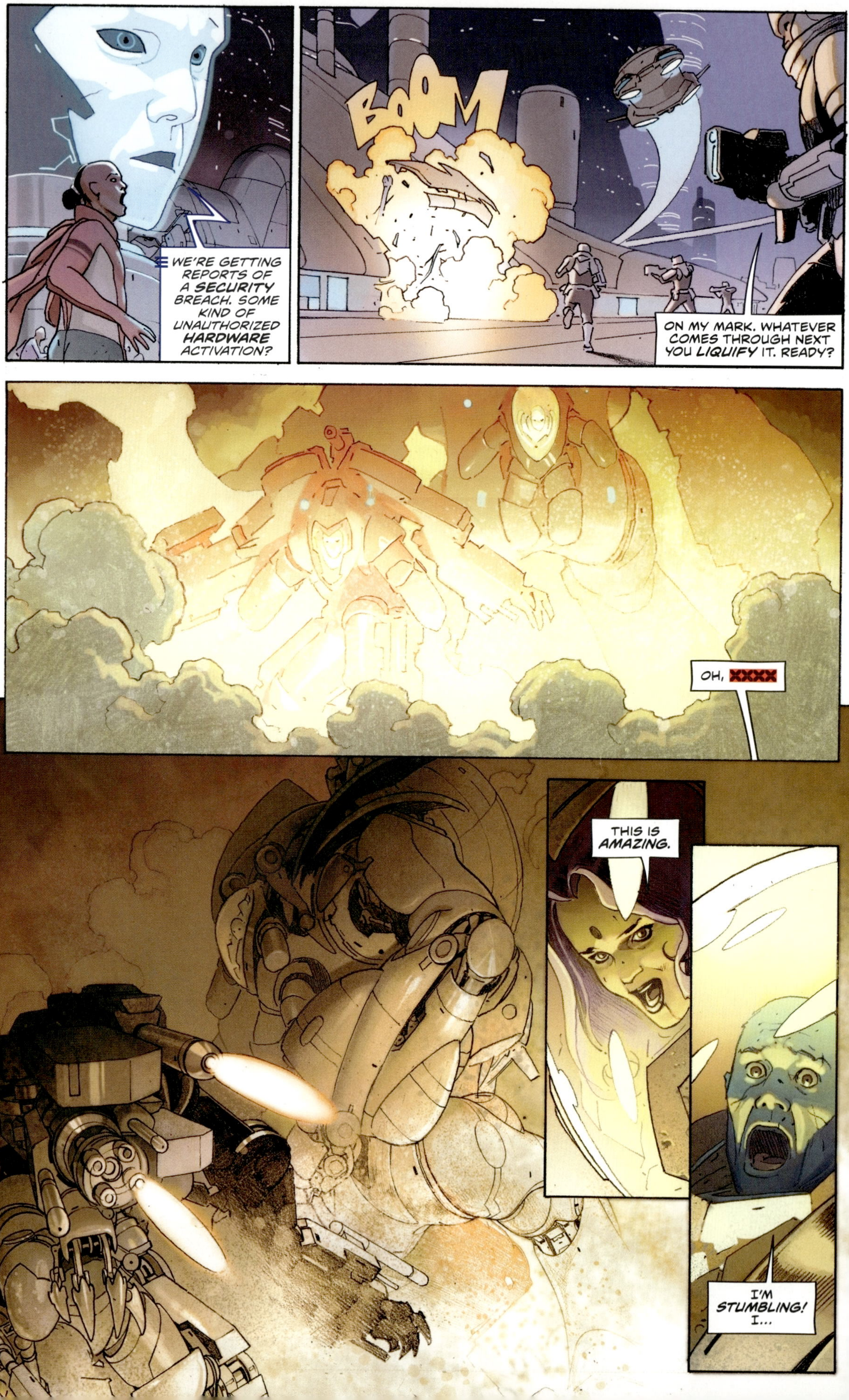
WE'RE GETTING REPORTS OF A SECURITY BREACH. SOME KIND OF UNAUTHORIZED HARDWARE ACTIVATION?
BOOM
ON MY MARK. WHATEVER COMES THROUGH NEXT YOU LIQUIFY IT. READY?
OH, XXXX
THIS IS AMAZING.
I'M STUMBLING! I...

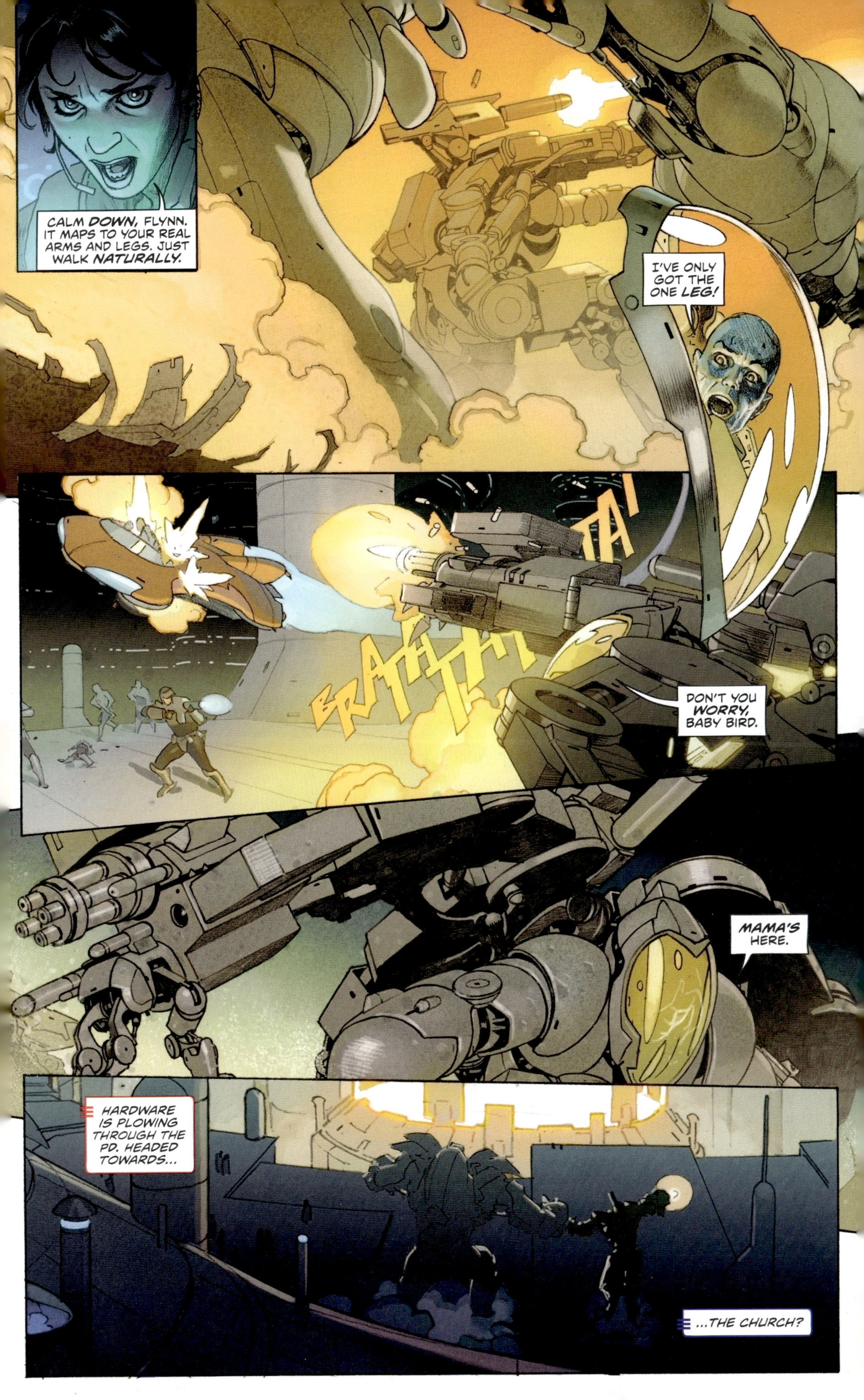

CALM DOWN, FLYNN. IT MAPS TO YOUR REAL ARMS AND LEGS. JUST WALK NATURALLY.
I'VE ONLY GOT THE ONE LEG!
TA!
BRATATATA
DON'T YOU WORRY, BABY BIRD.
MAMA'S HERE.
HARDWARE IS PLOWING THROUGH THE PD. HEADED TOWARDS...
...THE CHURCH?

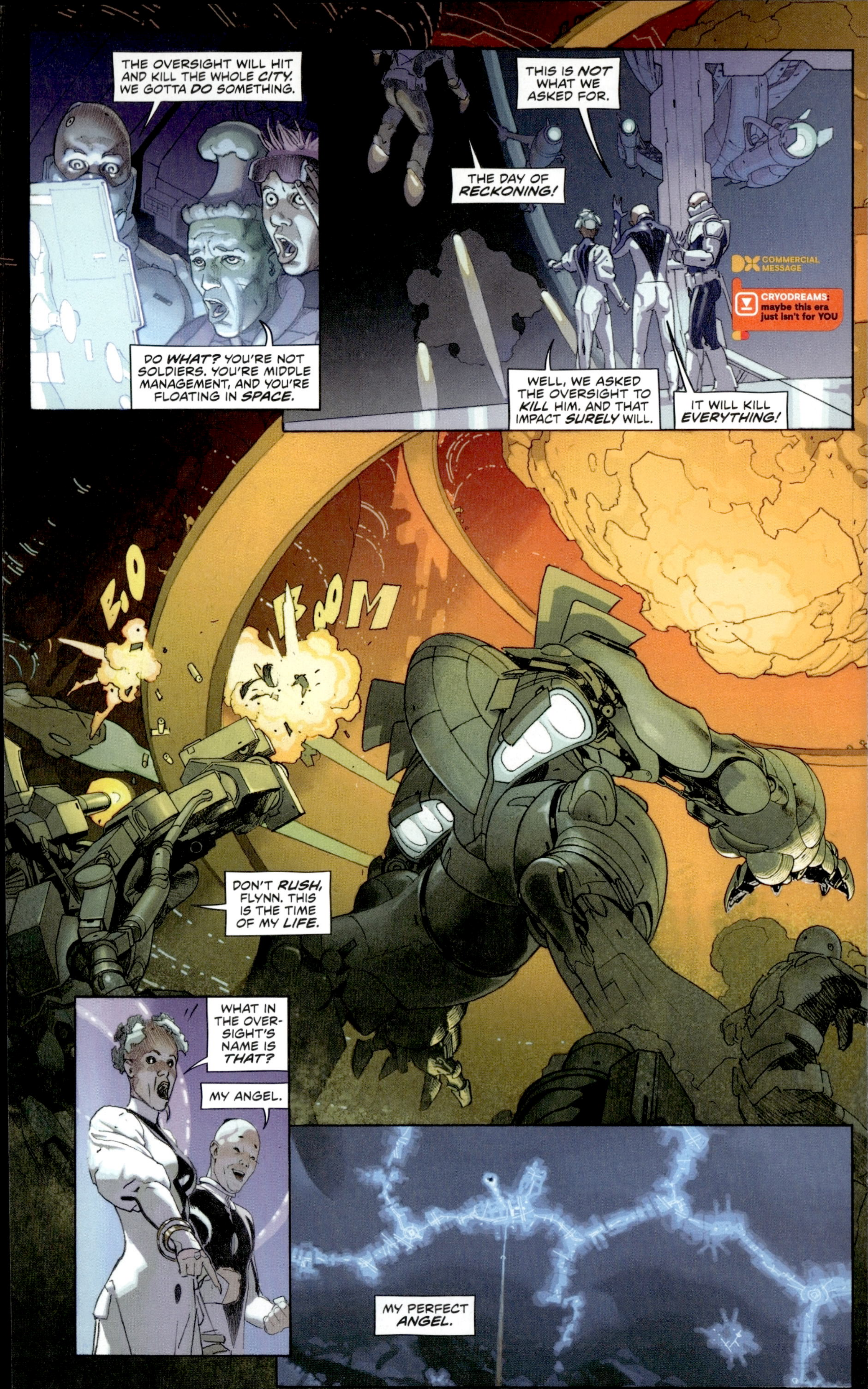
THE OVERSIGHT WILL HIT AND KILL THE WHOLE CITY. WE GOTTA DO SOMETHING.
DO WHAT? YOU'RE NOT SOLDIERS. YOU'RE MIDDLE MANAGEMENT, AND YOU'RE FLOATING IN SPACE.
THIS IS NOT WHAT WE ASKED FOR.
THE DAY OF RECKONING!
COMMERCIAL MESSAGE
CRYODREAMS: maybe this era just isn't for YOU
WELL, WE ASKED THE OVERSIGHT TO KILL HIM. AND THAT IMPACT SURELY WILL.
IT WILL KILL EVERYTHING!
BOOM
DON'T RUSH, FLYNN. THIS IS THE TIME OF MY LIFE.
WHAT IN THE OVER-SIGHT'S NAME IS THAT?
MY ANGEL.
MY PERFECT ANGEL.

WE HAVE NEW REPORTS NOW OF A STOLEN SPACECRAFT BREACHING THE CITY...?
THIS IS THE WILDEST CIRCUS I'VE EVER SEEN.
FFWOOOO
EVER IN YOUR SERVICE.

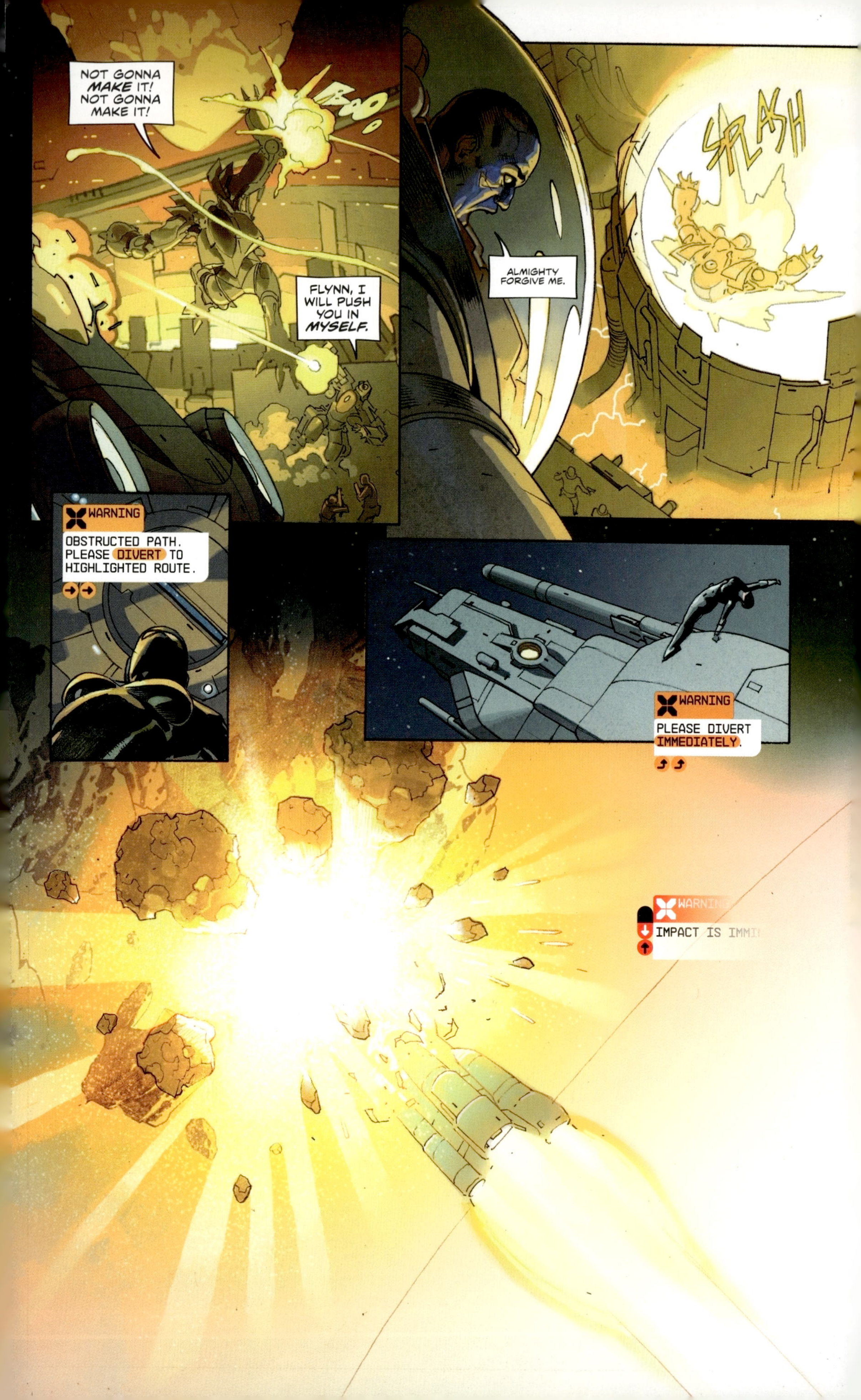
NOT GONNA MAKE IT! NOT GONNA MAKE IT!
BOO
FLYNN, I WILL PUSH YOU IN MYSELF.
ALMIGHTY FORGIVE ME.
SPLASH
WARNING
OBSTRUCTED PATH. PLEASE DIVERT TO HIGHLIGHTED ROUTE.
WARNING
PLEASE DIVERT IMMEDIATELY.
IMPACT IS IMMI

COMMERCIAL
MESSAGE
CHERRY
COMBAT
For times
like these.

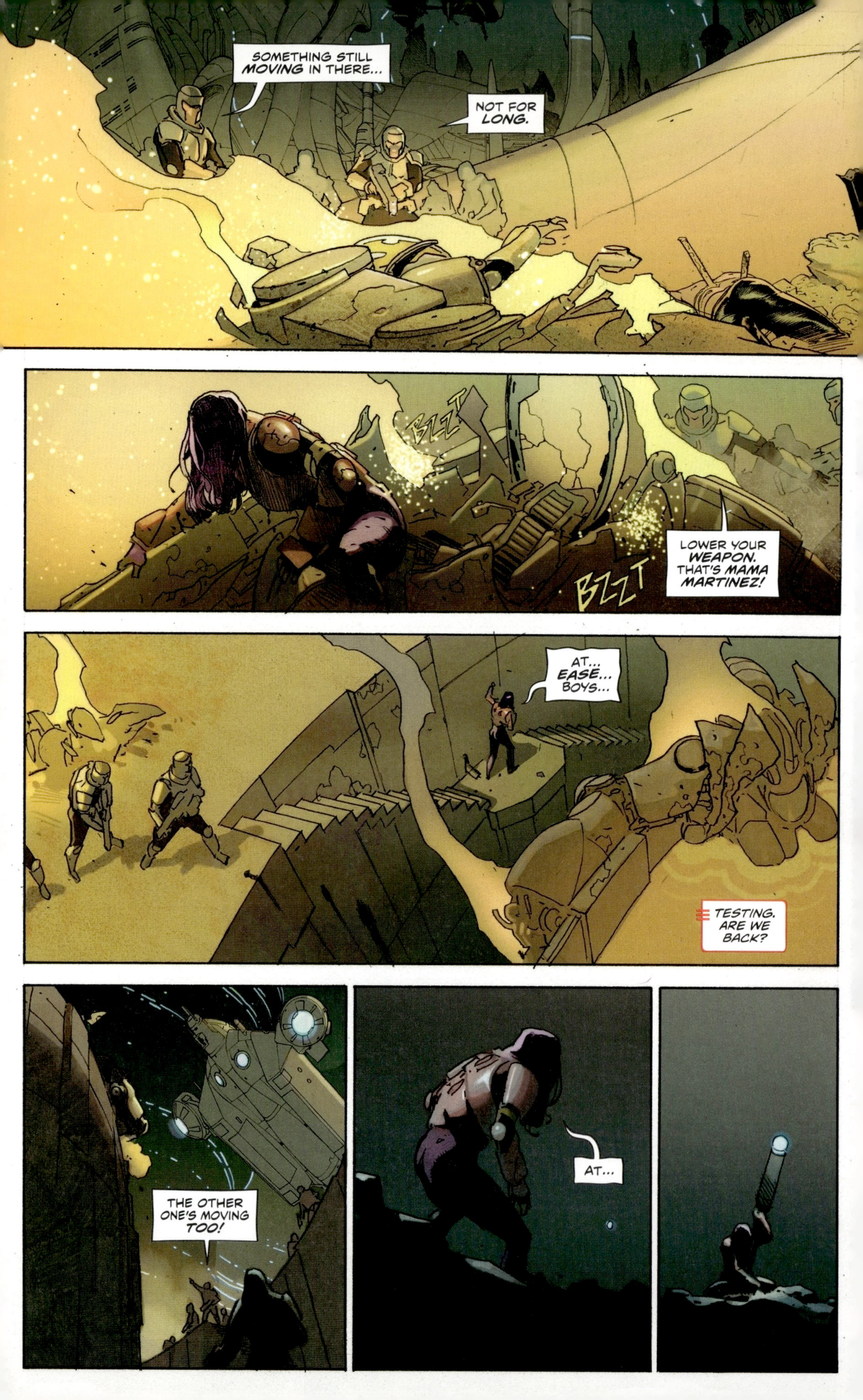
SOMETHING STILL MOVING IN THERE...
NOT FOR LONG.
BZZT
BZZT
LOWER YOUR WEAPON. THAT'S MAMA MARTINEZ!
AT... EASE... BOYS...
TESTING. ARE WE BACK?
THE OTHER ONE'S MOVING TOO!
AT...

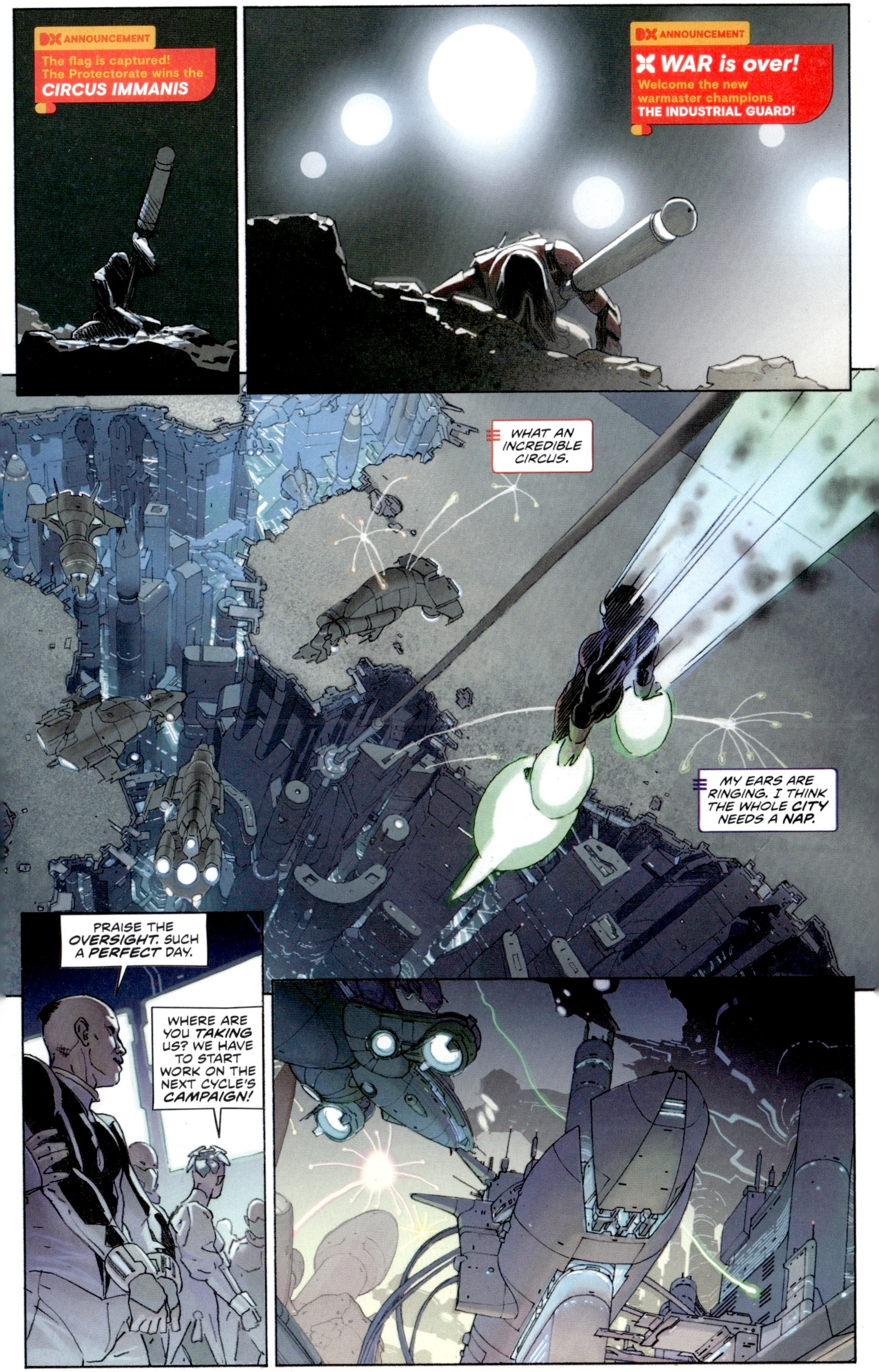

ANNOUNCEMENT
The flag is captured! The Protectorate wins the CIRCUS IMMANIS
ANNOUNCEMENT
WAR is over! Welcome the new warmaster champions THE INDUSTRIAL GUARD!
WHAT AN INCREDIBLE CIRCUS.
MY EARS ARE RINGING. I THINK THE WHOLE CITY NEEDS A NAP.
PRAISE THE OVERSIGHT. SUCH A PERFECT DAY.
WHERE ARE YOU TAKING US? WE HAVE TO START WORK ON THE NEXT CYCLE'S CAMPAIGN!

WHATEVER HAPPENED TO DEVI?
THERE!
I DON'T THINK SHE'S MOVING...
VITALS ARE BAD.
COOLANT. I SAID I NEED COOLANT!
SHE'S CONSCIOUS! MAJOR, CAN YOU HEAR ME?
DID WE...
WE WON.
THEY WON.
WITHOUT EITHER OF US.

SO WHAT'S NEXT FOR SATTA FLYNN?
WHAT'S NEXT FOR YOU?
MAYBE JUST THIS. MAYBE NOW WE'RE JUST PEOPLE WHO STARE AT THE MOON.
DON'T YOU RUIN THIS.
YOU SAVED EVERY ONE OF US. YOU DESTROYED THE ASTEROID.
YOU CAN'T KILL AN ASTEROID.
I JUST KNOCKED IT OUT OF THE PATH OF THE--

END
BROADCAST.

INFO MESSAGE

→VS COVER GALLERY_

VARIANT COVERS WITH ART FROM ESAD RIBIC/ DAN PANOSIAN/ JAE LEE/ AND DESIGN BY TOM MULLER

IVÁN BRANDON
ESAD RIBIĆ
With NIC KLEIN
#1
IMAGE
COMICS.COM
$3.99
image
RIBIĆ+
MULLER

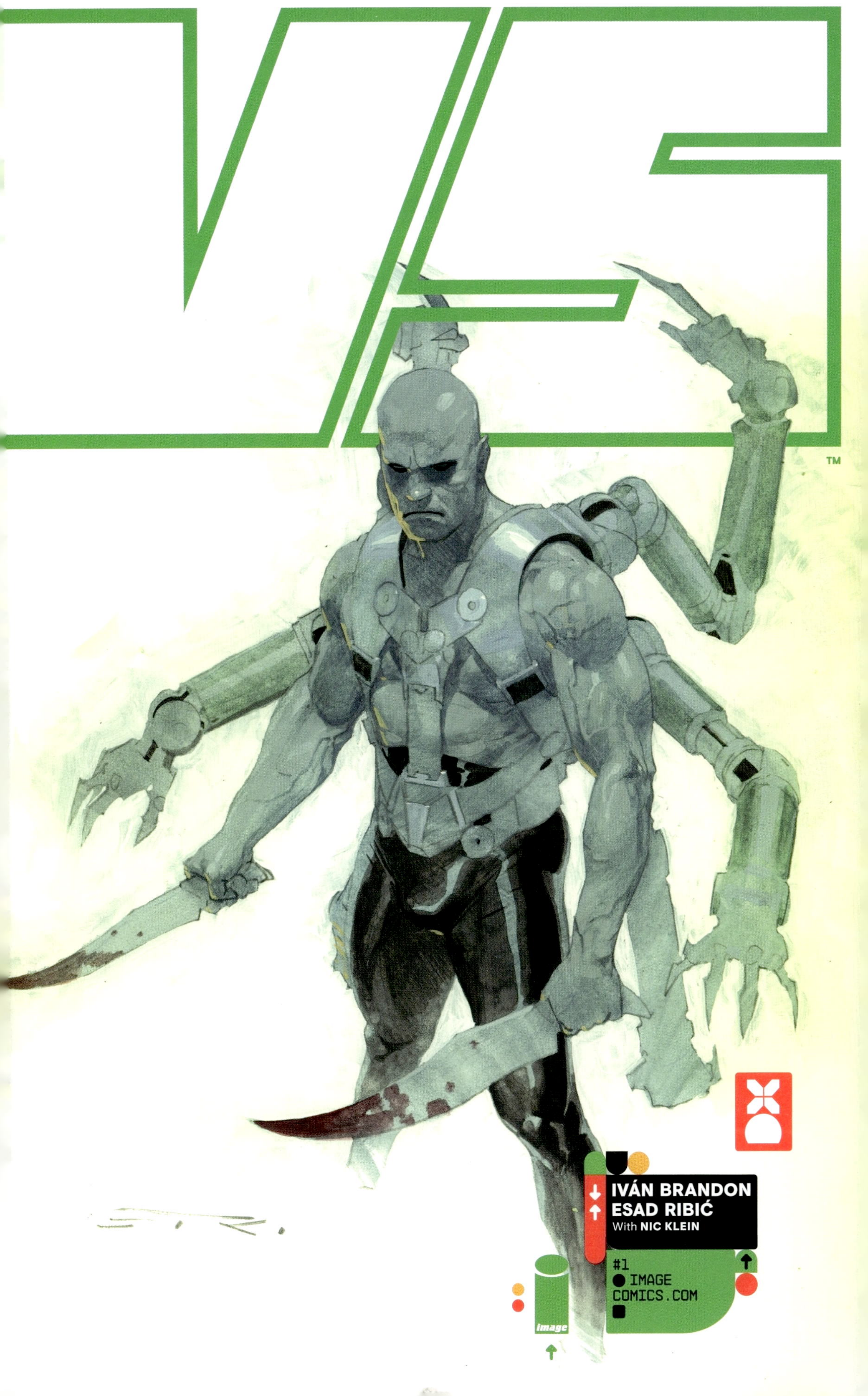
VS
IVÁN BRANDON
ESAD RIBIĆ
With NIC KLEIN
#1
IMAGE
COMICS.COM
image

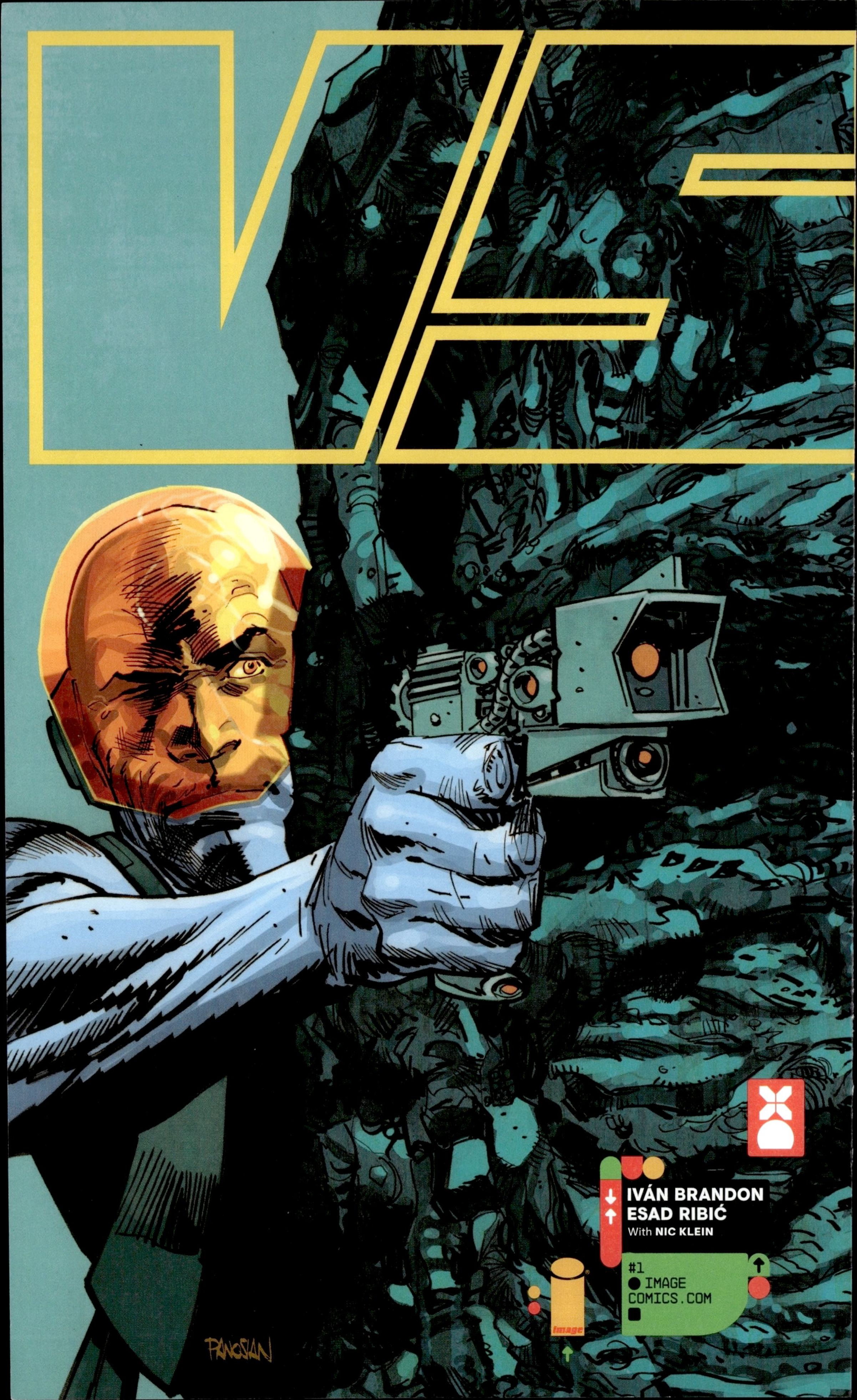
IVÁN BRANDON
ESAD RIBIĆ
With NIC KLEIN
#1
IMAGE
COMICS.COM
image

IVÁN BRANDON
ESAD RIBIĆ
With NIC KLEIN
#1
IMAGE
COMICS.COM
image

IVÁN BRANDON
ESAD RIBIĆ
With NIC KLEIN
#2
IMAGE
COMICS.COM
$3.99
image
RIBIĆ+
MULLER

#3
IMAGE
COMICS.COM
$3.99
IVÁN BRANDON
ESAD RIBIĆ
With NIC KLEIN
RIBIĆ+
MULLER

#4
IMAGE
COMICS.COM
$3.99
IVÁN BRANDON
ESAD RIBIC
With NIC KLEIN

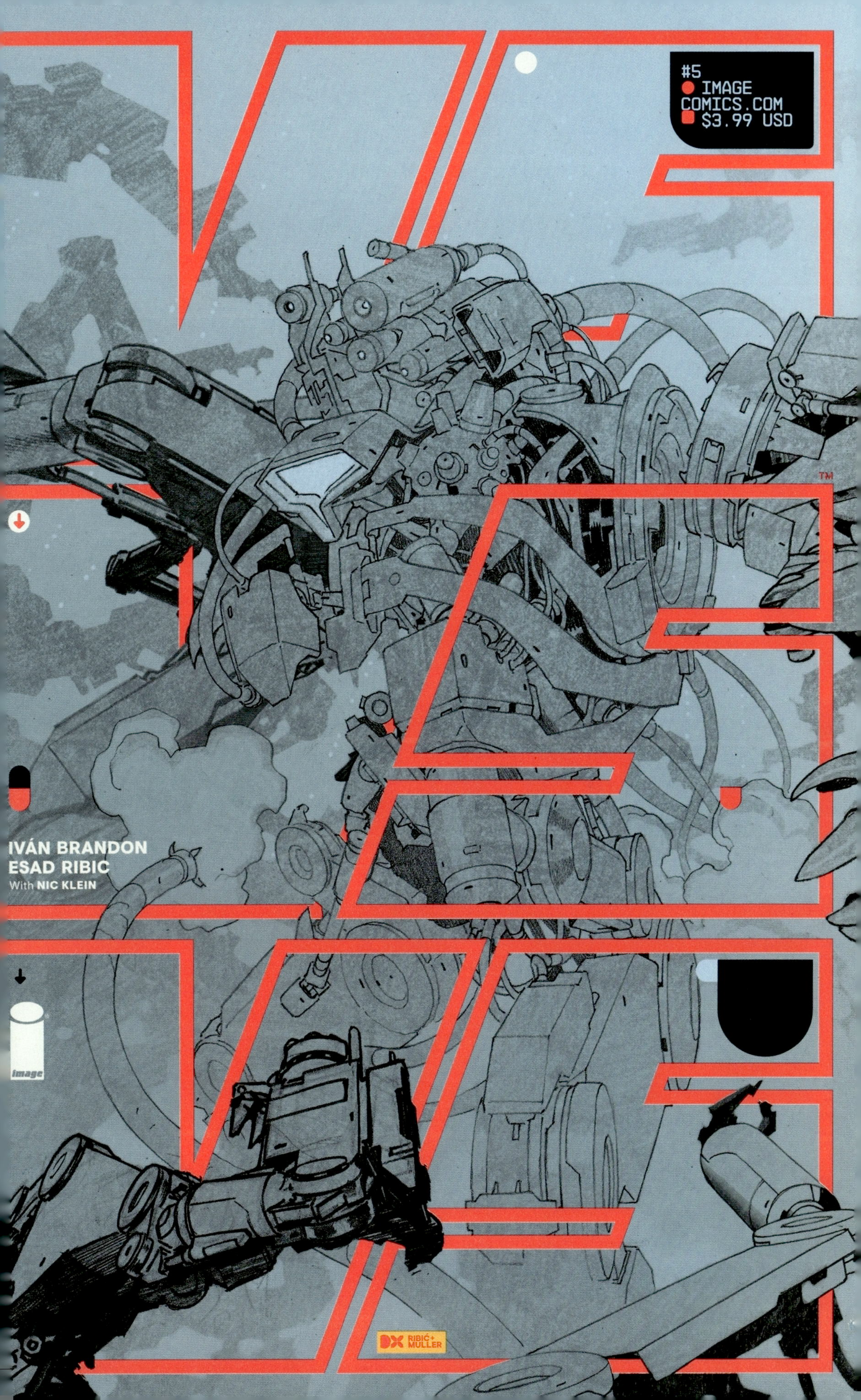
#5
IMAGE
COMICS.COM
$3.99 USD
IVÁN BRANDON
ESAD RIBIC
With NIC KLEIN
image
RIBIĆ+
MULLER

DX INFO MESSAGE

→IMAGE COMICS, INC.

VS, VOLUME 1. FIRST PRINTING. AUGUST 2018. PUBLISHED BY IMAGE COMICS, INC. OFFICE OF PUBLICATION: 2701 NW VAUGHN ST., SUITE 780, PORTLAND, OR 97210. PRINTED IN THE USA. FOR INFORMATION REGARDING THE CPSIA ON THIS PRINTED MATERIAL CALL: 203-595-3636 AND PROVIDE REFERENCE #RICH-806805. CONTACT: LAW OFFICES OF HARRIS M. MILLER II, P.C. (RIGHTSINQUIRIES@GMAIL.COM). ISBN: 978-1-5343-0693-6.